The fire within . . .

A parachute jump gone horribly wrong nearly put an end to Hunter Buchanan's smokejumper career. But with his body on the mend, the rugged firefighter is ready to get back to Oregon's Redmond Air Center and his training. Except, while he's conquered his physical injuries, he hasn't been able to do the same for his panic attacks. Enter Charlotte Jones, aka Charlie, the trainer who tames his tension like nobody's business. It doesn't hurt that she's easy on the eyes. Or that she stirs a hunger in him to deal with just about anything in order to be the man she needs . . .

After four years of hiding from a violent man in her past, Charlie is ready to face the world again. She knows this has more than a little to do with the potent mix of strength and vulnerability she's found in Hunter's arms. But when a dangerous encounter convinces her the worst isn't behind her, she'll have to decide if she's strong enough to accept Hunter's help— and his love . . .

Books by Marnee Blake

Smokejumpers series
Crave the Heat
Tempt the Flames
Risk the Burn

Published by Kensington Publishing Corporation

Risk the Burn

Smokejumpers

Marnee Blake

LYRICAL PRESS
Kensington Publishing Corp.
www.kensingtonbooks.com

LYRICAL PRESS BOOKS are published by
Kensington Publishing Corp.
119 West 40th Street
New York, NY 10018

All Kensington titles, imprints, and distributed lines are available at special quantity discounts for bulk purchases for sales promotion, premiums, fund-raising, educational, or institutional use.

Special book excerpts or customized printings can also be created to fit specific needs. For details, write or phone the office of the Kensington Sales Manager: Kensington Publishing Corp., 119 West 40th Street, New York, NY 10018. Attn. Sales Department. Phone: 1-800-221-2647.

Lyrical Press and Lyrical Press logo Reg. U.S. Pat. & TM Off.

First Electronic Edition: August 2019
eISBN-13: 978-1-5161-0770-4
eISBN-10: 1-5161-0770-5

First Print Edition: August 2019
ISBN-13: 978-1-5161-0773-5
ISBN-10: 1-5161-0773-X

Printed in the United States of America

Chapter One

The front door to Myers and Long Physical Therapy was unlocked when Charlie Jones yanked on it, confirming that her boss was already here and had opened for her. Which meant she was even later than she'd originally thought.

Sweeping through the workout area where she and the other physical therapists ran their clients through their exercises, she hurried into her minuscule office and dropped her purse on the desk. The contents spilled all over, a handful of her belongings rolling off the side and onto the floor. Damn, why hadn't she stopped for a second to close the thing? Because she'd been late, that's why. As usual. And per the norm, because she hadn't taken the time to do things the right way, she was stuck tossing what felt like every lip gloss and pen she owned back into her bag.

"Les, I'm here," she called, pushing her wallet into a space that had held it moments earlier but didn't seem big enough for it now. "Sorry I'm late."

"Please." Her boss, Leslie Myers, stepped into the doorway of the bathroom, a small grin on her face. "No you aren't." She pressed her fist against the doorframe, swaying.

"You're right." Her perpetual lateness was a running joke between them. Leslie always said Charlie's internal clock was permanently set to five minutes behind everyone else's. Charlie narrowed her eyes, studying her boss. "You don't look so good."

Leslie pressed her hand against her stomach, her face pale. "I don't feel so good."

Abandoning her purse, Charlie hurried to the watercooler, removed a paper cone cup, and filled it. "Why are you here, then, girl?"

Creeping forward, Leslie dropped into a chair, waving off Charlie's offered water. "The interview. It's this morning."

That's right. How had she forgotten?

The town's newspaper had been following the recovery of a local smokejumper. After a parachute malfunction, Hunter Buchanan had been forced to drop out of last year's smokejumper training class. A concussion, a broken arm and leg, and a handful of other life-threatening injuries had made for a long road to recovery—a path that had led him to Myers and Long. Today, though, would be his final physical therapy treatment, only two weeks before he was scheduled to join this year's smokejumper training class. The paper wanted to be here to witness his triumph. Or rather, they wanted to be here to wrap up their feel-good story with a pretty bow.

"What time?" she asked. If this was something Leslie ate and the interview was later this afternoon, she could still do it.

Leslie's eyes widened. Though she'd appeared close to death a second ago, she was up and running to the bathroom with Olympic-sprinter speed. The sound of retching followed.

She hurried after her boss, but Leslie pulled the bathroom door closed behind her. The hollow wood door did nothing to mask her sickness.

Charlie pressed her hand to her forehead, glancing at the clock. It was ten after nine in the morning. If this was the beginning of some sort of stomach virus, those were never nice enough to finish up fast. No doubt Leslie would be choking down crackers and fighting nausea tomorrow at this time.

Which left Charlie in charge of reporters, maybe a photographer, and definitely one sexy-as-hell Hunter Buchanan.

Not that she was supposed to have paid attention to that, because it was completely unprofessional. Still, it would be hard not to notice.

The truth was that she'd been aware of how sexy Hunter was even before he became a client at Myers and Long. His sister, Meg, was her closest friend here in Oregon, so she'd casually met him a few times. For example, Meg's birthday party two years ago had been in a restaurant, so she hadn't expected him to mingle too much, but aloof and gorgeous was her brand of hot. She'd watched him all night, wondering what his story was and being way too attracted to him.

When he'd been the victim of a jump gone wrong during smokejumper training last year, her heart had broken for him, Meg, and their family. After his stint in rehab, he'd been discharged and Meg had referred him to Myers and Long, where Charlie worked.

Charlie had kept her distance, asking Leslie to take him as a client. First, she was his sister's good friend. She wouldn't be breaking any ethical guidelines by working with him, but she worried it might be awkward. Physical therapy was hands-on, and hanging out with Meg after having her hands all over her best friend's brother might be weird.

But, more important, Charlie didn't trust how much she might like being that physical with Hunter Buchanan. His first few appointments had solidified the rightness of her choice. Every time he walked through their doors, she was hyperaware of him and the energy he brought with him. There was something there, some connection between them. Or maybe it was only her, because she doubted there were many women alive who wouldn't notice how gorgeous he was.

Either way, it was best that she stayed away.

Except now, with Leslie losing whatever she'd eaten for breakfast in the other room, she might not have a choice but to break the self-enforced distance she'd put between them.

Sauntering over to the bathroom door, but keeping a safe distance from having to witness any real vomiting, she offered, "Leslie? Are you okay?"

"No," her friend moaned. "I'm dying."

"Oh God." Charlie pressed her finger to her brow. "I'm calling Kyle."

She had no idea if Leslie agreed to getting her husband involved, because her response was more of a groan than a real word. Charlie retrieved her phone from her bag, sifting through the contacts until she hit Kyle's number, and pressed send. By the time Leslie shuffled out of the bathroom, her husband was on his way.

"Are you sure you can manage this?" Leslie asked, scanning the office.

Charlie patted her on the shoulder, offering a reassuring smile. She had no idea, but there was nothing to be done about it now. "Tracy will be here in a little bit. We'll go through the appointments, figure out what can be rescheduled, and I'll juggle the rest. Don't worry about it. I can handle this."

Her boss offered her a wan grin as her husband pulled up on the curb outside. Thank goodness he only worked a few miles away. "What about the interview?"

"I got this." Charlie hoped she looked more confident than she felt. "Just feel better."

Leslie waved on her way out the door, sliding into the passenger seat. Her husband closed the door behind her, concern on his face. Charlie smiled. Kyle clearly adored Leslie. They were a cute pair.

But as they pulled away, foreboding settled in her gut.

She could definitely manage any of the appointments. The interview, though?

A shudder ran down her spine.

It wasn't talking to the reporter. She wasn't shy, so she'd never been afraid to talk to anyone. But the photographer who might accompany her? Terrifying.

For the past few years, she'd done everything in her power to stay off the internet and out of the public eye. That's what a person did when she'd gone through the trouble to change her name and start a new life a thousand miles from home.

There was nothing she could do about it now, not if she didn't want to let Leslie down. She'd try her hardest to stay out of pictures and hope for the best. After all, it had been three years. She had no idea what Joshua was doing now, but surely he'd long ago forgotten about her.

It would be fine. No sweat. She'd remain professional working with a man she found insanely hot while trying to keep her face obscured from any cameras.

How hard could it be?

* * * *

As Hunter Buchanan parked his SUV in front of the Myers and Long in Bend, Oregon, he caught sight of the news van at the corner. The morning traffic around him faded.

Rubbing his now sweaty palms on the thighs of his workout pants, he closed his eyes, inhaling deeply. In one of the self-help books he'd devoured in his search to manage his anxiety, he'd read that rhythmic breathing could help stave off the panic. He'd watched a bunch of meditation videos and even spent time at a couple of yoga classes, trying to master his breath.

It was supposed to be all zen and shit. And it worked. Sometimes.

Now, apparently, wasn't one of those times.

In through the nose, out through the mouth.

It wasn't like this was the first of the interviews. But the entire exclusive and story hadn't been his idea. Mitch had suggested that he talk with the paper, that it would go a long way in removing some of the scandalous taint from his accident.

Not that it had been an accident. Which was part of the problem. Things didn't get any more titillating for the public than a man causing the near death of his brother in his attempt to kill the man he blamed for his father's death.

It was the stuff of soap operas. All it had needed was a secret baby.

Which was exactly why he'd agreed to this human interest story in the first place. If the public believed he had recovered, that he'd triumphed over the insane circumstances of last spring, then maybe his family could move on.

More, he needed to persuade Mitch that he had, in fact, recovered. Because the Redmond Air Center manager still hadn't agreed to let him join the rookie training class in a few weeks.

Which explained the sweaty palms and racing heart. Today, he needed to be extra convincing.

Yanking the keys from the ignition, he grabbed his duffel, climbed out, and locked the doors, pinning a confident smile on his face. He strolled across the parking lot and tried to ignore what remained of the aches in his bones, but there was moisture in the air. Since he'd broken his arm and leg, they nagged at him when rain threatened.

He was greeted by the receptionist, Tracy, as soon as he walked in. "Morning, Mr. Buchanan."

Hunter had asked her to call him by his first name three different times. She never did. "Hey, Tracy." He glanced around, bracing to be bombarded by the reporter from the *Gazette*. "Leslie here?"

"She actually isn't, Mr. Buchanan. She had to go home unexpectedly. You'll be working with Charlie Jones."

Lifting his eyebrows, he continued his scan of the physical therapy office before his gaze snagged on Charlie, talking with the woman from the *Gazette*.

Compact, with short brown curls and a huge, bubbly personality, Charlie smiled at Lena Rodriguez, the veteran *Gazette* reporter, before catching his eye. Same as always, something zinged between them, even as her grin dimmed. He wondered if she did that on purpose. Every time he'd hung out with Charlie Jones, one of his sister's good friends, he got the feeling that something about him rubbed her the wrong way. For someone with such an open smile, someone who put everyone around her immediately at ease, well, it was obvious when a guy wasn't included in the easy camaraderie.

Had he offended her somewhere along the line? He couldn't think of anything. When he'd asked Meg, she'd told him he was nuts. Maybe she was right, but he'd been watching women his whole life. Something about Charlie was on edge when he was near.

In response, he usually steered clear of her. He had no desire to make her uncomfortable, so he gave her plenty of space. No choice now, though. How he came across in this interview would hopefully tip the scales for Mitch. It might mean the difference between whether he got to join rookie training and whether he was stuck working as a hotshot again.

The tightness in his chest had sharpened, and his heart rate had picked up. It became hard to breathe, and he took a sharp detour to the nearest open door—Leslie's office.

Pulling the door shut as softly as he could, desperate not to draw attention to himself, he tried to slow his breath. He tried to convince himself he wasn't dying even though everything in his physiology said he was, in fact, going to die. Or, best-case scenario, that something awful was about to happen.

Pacing out of sight of the window, he pressed his palm to his chest, the hard pounding of his heartbeat banging against it. He wanted it to end, would do about anything to take the pain out. But despite his efforts at logic, he was forced to ride along as his brain offered him worst-case scenarios. Like, that he was having a heart attack or a stroke. That he'd suffocate, unable to pull in a full breath, even though he was standing upright that very moment.

The door opened and Charlie stepped in. Her dark eyes—the ones with the laugh lines he'd admired—scanned him, taking in the situation. Then she stood next to him, gripping his arm. "What's going on?"

"I'm fine," he gasped out. "Just give me. A moment."

She rested her other hand on his back. It might have been his imagination, but the heat and firmness of the touch took the sharp edges off his breath. As if it loosened his chest somehow.

Her fingers gripped his wrist, and her gaze went to the clock. She counted under her breath. "Your pulse is nearly two hundred beats a minute. You're not fine."

He pulled his hand from her grasp, shaking his head.

"It'll pass. Just give me a second." With her here distracting him, he could almost believe that was true.

"Do you know what's happening?" Her brow had dropped, and her seriousness was at odds with her usual smile and upbeat personality.

He didn't want to tell her anything. This had been his secret these past months, something he'd dealt with. Not because he was ashamed, but because he needed them to stop. Smokejumping and panic attacks didn't mix. If he didn't tell anyone, it almost felt like he could pretend they weren't real. A figment of his imagination or some kind of nightmare.

Except now he couldn't exactly pretend. Either he confessed to her and trusted she'd keep his secret or he took his chances with the reporter and photographer outside.

It was a no-brainer.

"Panic. Attack," he gasped out, one hand still on his chest, the other on his waist.

Chapter Two

There was absolutely nothing in Hunter's chart about panic attacks or anxiety.

She wasn't an expert on anxiety disorders or panic attacks, at least nothing past the one or two panic attacks she'd had in her own life. Maybe this was a one-and-done thing for him.

But if he recognized that it was, indeed, a panic attack, it probably wasn't his first one.

Even as questions spun in her head, she did nothing. If she were him, in that moment, she wouldn't want anyone throwing a zillion questions in her face. In her experience, in the worst situations, the ones that she'd wished to just be alone and silent, those were the times when someone or many someones would throw questions at her like darts, expecting her to think, to perform, to stop acting so strange. Except it always seemed that they didn't care as much about her as they cared about themselves. They wanted to stop feeling worried or uncomfortable. They acted as if it was her job in those moments to take away their concern.

So she stood quiet, waiting. The only sound was his rapid breathing, so she breathed as slowly and completely as she could. She closed her eyes, hoping he'd latch onto her calm. When it seemed to be working, when his inhale and exhale became more even, she realized she'd been running her hand along his back. In the now-silent room, with both of them breathing normally, awareness crept through her, centered on her fingers, still pressed into the warm muscles along his spine.

As casually as she could manage, she retrieved her fingers, clasping them with her other hand in front of her and attempting her most professional smile. "Better?"

He dropped the hand he'd been pressing against his chest, leaned against Leslie's desk on both fists, and nodded. As his head dropped, she used the moment to step back, trying to find some distance from him in her boss's minuscule office.

Well, now what?

A sideways glance out the window in Leslie's door revealed that Ms. Rodriguez and her photographer, Spike, were waiting, their heads together, chatting. Unless she claimed that Hunter had been struck by lightning, run over by a rhino, or coincidentally got the same nasty flu that Leslie had, she needed to get out there with him. Looking him over—the sweat on his forehead, the pale cheeks—she might be able to sell a flu.

She considered approaching the reporter, asking her to withhold her name and photo. But that would mean explaining to Hunter her past issues, potentially open herself up to questions from Leslie about why she'd needed to pull back in the interview. All of that would lead to lots of explanations she preferred not to give.

It had been years. Surely the danger was over now, right?

"You okay now?" she asked. The stark terror had left his face, and his color was returning. When he finally straightened, he looked like the Hunter she'd met before. Strong, confident, and capable.

Sexy as hell.

He nodded, running his hand over his sandy brown hair. The move should have made it messy, but somehow he made disheveled look good.

She sighed. She needed to get ahold of herself.

Awkwardness settled over her. Now that he was more normal-looking and she was more aware of how hot he was again, she didn't know what to say. But standing together in Leslie's office could only get weirder the longer they did it without talking, so she gave conversation a shot. "So…I'm going to be your therapist today."

One side of his mouth quirked up. "Physical or psychological?"

She exhaled on a laugh. "Well, one I'm qualified to do, the other not so much."

"Right." He glanced toward the reporter. "Leslie's not here?"

"Sick." She scanned him again. "Are you sick?" The question was tentative and even the smallest bit hopeful. Did it make her a bad person to be wishing that a mystery virus might get her out of this interview situation?

Probably.

His smirk said he agreed. "No, I'm fine."

"That's good. Great," she offered, too fast for either of them to believe her. "Then I guess we should get out there. They're waiting for us."

"I know." He rubbed his palms on his pant legs.

"Do you need me to stall for you?" Honestly, she didn't know what to do. "Or will you be able to go out there in a second?"

Tugging on his shirt, he squared his shoulders. "I think it's good."

"Are you sure?" When he inhaled, she continued on, quickly. "I mean, do you have those a lot? You seemed to know—"

"No, no. Not at all."

"So that was your first one?"

"No." He waved her off, shaking his head. "But they're going to want to talk, you know, about everything. About the accident, and about the fall. About the injuries and the pain, and how my healing has gone." He rattled it all off, like the stuff he was talking about was normal conversation for him. "But what bugs me is they ask about my family. About my mom, my sister, about how everyone's doing, and I need to smile and pretend it's totally fine that they're invading my loved ones' privacy when I really want to tell them to fuck off."

She blinked. "Right." She pressed her lips together, releasing them with a soft popping sound. "Well, I can see how that might make things awkward."

He laughed, the sound surprised, bursting out of him. The rumble struck her low in the stomach.

Sweet baby Jesus.

As his bright blue eyes met hers, he grinned. "Don't worry, I'm not going to tell them that. I have it together now. Thanks."

He gathered his things, and she paused before turning the doorknob. "If you hate doing this, why did you agree to it in the first place?" It definitely hadn't been Leslie's idea. Leslie didn't like the spotlight, and she would hate the interruption.

"It wasn't my idea. The head of the smokejumper base thought it might be a good way to take some of the pressure off everyone. If I talked about what happened, how I was doing, then it would take some of the mystery out of it." He shrugged. "You know. Everyone loves a scandal."

"Were people bothering you?"

His eyes widened. "After the accident? Of course."

It made sense. Hunter's brother had caused his accident while trying to frighten another smokejumper on their team. Then, his uncle had killed himself because of his own guilt about his part in the death of his brother—Hunter's father. The world, at least their little slice of the world, would find that scandalous and need to know every detail.

"Did they bother Meg?" Had her friend been dealing with nagging reporters and said nothing?

"You mean Meg my sister, the one dating the man my brother was trying to hurt?" He blew a raspberry. "Funny."

Charlie pressed her palm to her forehead. "Why didn't she tell me?" They were friends. Good friends. Good enough for Meg to have said something, vented, whatever.

More important, she should have checked on her friend. She should have guessed what was going on.

Meg had been busy with Lance, her new boyfriend, and Charlie hadn't wanted to intrude. They looked so cozy together. She'd felt like a third wheel. But that didn't excuse her from making sure she was okay. "I should have checked on her."

Hunter tilted his head. "She knew you were thinking of her, I'm sure of it. Besides, you know Meg. She would hate people fussing over her."

"Doesn't mean I shouldn't have done it."

He grinned. "You're a good friend."

"I just told you I had no idea that people were swarming on your sister, a woman I consider a close friend. You aren't listening."

"Maybe. But I think I've got it right." He nudged his head to the door. "So, I guess I have to do this."

She wrinkled her nose in the direction of the intruders in her office. "Are you going to be okay with them?"

The smile slipped from his face. A hint of his earlier panic flashed in his eyes, and every hope that she'd be able to slink into the background died.

Leslie had left Hunter's discharge papers with her. Hunter was done with his physical therapy. By all benchmarks and milestones, he was physically healed. After today, he'd walk out of this office, off to do whatever he planned next with his amazingly toned and gorgeous body.

But that meant the reporter out there was going to ask him if he really was healed. That would lead to prying questions. She could imagine all the ways they'd try to get him to admit how affected he still was by the accident. The interview was voyeurism at its worst, all the reasons people watched reality shows. Sure, the public loved a happy ending. But for whatever reason, no one seemed to be able to look away from a car accident. There were many who would feed on any indication that he was still hurting.

She couldn't let him face that alone. More, she wouldn't. Not only because she was Meg's friend, though that was part of it. But also because everything about Hunter suggested he was a private person. And she was all too aware of what it felt like to have people staring at her, wondering if she was about to fall apart.

Memories of her direct experience with that surfaced, accompanied by the usual wash of terror.

She'd kept a low profile since moving to Bend a few years ago. She didn't have social media, and she avoided having her picture taken, afraid it would end up on the internet. Maybe she was paranoid, but there were ghosts she'd prefer to not find her.

It had been three years, though, and nothing had ever come up. Maybe she was making too much of it. Maybe she could truly put her past with Joshua behind her.

Either way, faced with Hunter's panic, she refused to let anything keep her from helping him. "I'll be there. In case you need me."

Outside, the reporter was waiting and, if they didn't hurry, she would be joined by a slew of other clients she needed to see today. They had to get this show on the road.

He masked whatever had been going through his mind. "No sweat. I've got this."

"Right." She chuckled. "Well, either way. I'll be there." She squeezed his forearm.

It had seemed like the natural thing to do. They were having a moment or something. Except as soon as she touched him, whatever friendly, us-against-the-world and we-got-this delusions she'd believed they were sharing slipped away, replaced by a whole lot of heat. At least on her part.

He wasn't wearing long sleeves, so as her grip loosened, her fingertips trailed against very warm, very toned muscle. The pads of her fingers tingled, and her breathing hitched. Her eyes met his, and connection zinged between them, lighting up a part of her brain she'd tried to pretend wasn't completely starved.

She was a physical therapist, so she had an appreciation of superior physiques. But that wasn't this.

No, this? This was the result of the neglected sexual libido of a twenty-six-year-old who hadn't slept with anyone in three long years.

She noticed hot guys all the time. At the gym, at the bars. It wasn't that Hunter was good-looking. This was something more than attraction. It was why she steered clear of him.

She dropped her hand, glancing away.

If being on the internet was scary, attraction to someone like Hunter was terrifying.

"We should get out there." Shifting back and away, she jerked her thumb toward the door.

"Yeah." Tilting his head, his brow crinkled, as if he was worried there was something wrong with her. "Let's go."

He opened the door first, ushering her through before striding out. Gone was any hint that he'd suffered from a panic attack only minutes earlier. He moved with the complete confidence and easy grace of a born athlete, someone in tip-top physical shape. Someone who believed the world was at their fingertips.

Either she'd imagined everything that had happened in the office or Hunter was more complicated than she'd given him credit for.

Which, of course, made him way more appealing.

"Ms. Rodriguez." He smiled, offering his hand. "It's good to see you again."

"Good morning, Mr. Buchanan." The reporter pushed her glasses up her nose, removing a recorder from her pocket. "It's good to see you as well. I'd hoped that we could talk for maybe a few minutes, and then you can run through your exercises while Spike grabs a few photos. After that, we should be able to wrap this all up." Her smile was overly bright, and she ran her gaze over Hunter. "You certainly look as if you're all healed up."

The comment struck Charlie wrong. Did she imagine the sexual innuendo? The reporter, her face smooth as she fiddled with her recorder, seemed innocent.

That it might be Charlie's own attraction to him assigning innuendo bothered her.

"I'll wait over here," Charlie said, motioning to her desk. "Is that okay, Mr. Buchanan?" She used the formal name because it matched the fake smile she'd pasted on her face.

He nodded to her but didn't bother to answer, his attention entirely on the pretty reporter. As if she hadn't just helped him through a panic attack and she wasn't putting herself at risk of being exposed on the internet for him.

That wasn't nice. It was her decision to help. It was the right thing to do, considering her friendship with his sister. It wasn't his fault that he didn't understand how dangerous this interview might be for her.

She retreated to her desk, doing her best to appear as if she wasn't hiding and praying that the next half an hour or so went as fast as possible.

Chapter Three

Fifteen minutes into the physical therapy checks, Charlie was ready to call it quits.

Not for herself. Once she'd fallen into her professional habits, she could hide more easily. She was comfortable with "physical therapist Charlie." Besides, Hunter's recovery appeared to have gone wonderfully. He had all the ranges of movement that were required for discharge. In fact, he was much further advanced than most of the patients she stopped seeing regularly. Some of that could be accounted for by insurance policies. Certain companies only paid for a limited number of treatments. But even some clients who completed the full stint recommended by their doctors didn't have the superior results Hunter exhibited.

He must have worked incredibly hard.

She could see it on his face. He wore determination like a uniform. His drive to get better, to be at peak performance, was in every efficient move he made. Some of the stretches had to hurt, even if residually. But he never grimaced, hiding the effort it must take him to complete each movement flawlessly.

Or he was hiding any strain from the reporter and her photographer.

Charlie gritted her teeth. Her initial assessment of Reporter Rodriguez had been dead-on. The woman was simultaneously watching Hunter for any indication that he was in pain and looking like she wanted to lick every square, sweaty inch of him. Both aspects of her personality were grating on Charlie's nerves.

She didn't have a whole lot of time to dwell on the reporter, though. She was busy trying to keep her face tilted and obscured when the photographer got close. But damn Spike seemed to be trying to get his shots from every angle. Because she didn't know exactly what direction he was shooting from, she tried to keep her face down. Maybe if she didn't look directly at the camera, her features would remain obscured.

At least that's what she hoped.

"How are you doing?" she whispered to Hunter, low enough that no one else would hear. Or they'd assume she was instructing. Probably helped that she wasn't looking at him.

"Peachy," he offered as quietly, through clenched teeth.

"I'm cutting this short." She managed the words while barely moving her lips, like a ventriloquist.

"Absolutely not," he gritted back. "We do it all."

What she wanted was to ignore him. Having an audience was not conducive to inspecting and walking through a discharge process. She'd prefer to do this later, after everyone left. But she understood why they couldn't. He'd already told them what he would be doing, so if they were paying close attention, they'd notice that the workout was shorter than expected.

She managed to walk him through the rest of the activities as quickly as possible. By the end, his shirt was drenched, sticking to his body, but his face was peaceful. As if he hadn't been working his ass off. When they finished, he wiped his forehead with the hem of his T-shirt, revealing a strip of tanned and chiseled abs. Not that she noticed. Even though Reporter Rodriguez definitely wasn't averting her eyes.

"All done," he told her, his smile so charming it hurt to look at it.

"How do you feel, Mr. Buchanan?" She might have asked him the question, but her eyes were on that six-pack.

"Back in fighting shape." He propped his hands on his hips, and if Charlie didn't know exactly how hard isolating those muscles must have been and how hard he pushed himself, she might have believed that the workout was no sweat.

"So you think you're ready to start smokejumper training in a few weeks?" Rodriguez held the recorder toward him, her face expectant.

"Absolutely."

Reporter Rodriguez twisted, turning the recorder toward her. Her too-astute gaze bored through her. "Ms. Jones. What is your prognosis?"

"I think that Mr. Buchanan is ready to be discharged." That was the professional opinion. But she couldn't help adding, "I also think that he can do whatever he puts his mind to."

"Do you believe that he's ready to try smokejumping again?"

Charlie wanted to smack her mild, prying, inquisitive face. "As far as we at Myers and Long are concerned, he's prepared to begin whatever activities he chooses."

"Even if it could find him back here again in your trusted care?"

Her outrage on his behalf ratcheted up. "I think that's assuming—"

"Interesting." Rodriguez cut her off, turning her recorder off with a press, pocketing it. A click sounded next to Charlie, as loud as a cannon blast. Spike and his Nikon were next to her. She glared. She'd tried to avoid him, but the guy was like a tick she couldn't shake.

As if Reporter Rodriguez had sent him some sort of silent signal, the two of them began to pack up their gear. Rodriguez smiled, offering them both her hand as Spike stowed his camera and lenses, zippering them all in with infinite care. "Thank you both for having us."

Charlie didn't see how she'd had a choice, but she tried for a smile. "I suppose it was a pleasure."

"Of course." Rodriguez's smile was too sweet. She turned to Hunter, looking him over again. "It was a pleasure to spend so much time with you. You have my number? In case you'd like to keep in touch?"

Again, Charlie wasn't sure if she imagined the innuendo. Hunter, though, continued his charming smile. She wondered if it hurt. "Of course. I have your card."

"Wonderful." She waved, following Spike. "I'll email you with a link when the piece appears online."

She didn't wait, only wiggled her fingers and floated past the receptionist, out the door.

Charlie glared after her. "She's awful."

Hunter smirked. "Like a pretty viper."

She laughed, but she couldn't help feeling as if the reporter had taken her peace of mind with her.

* * * *

Hunter had never been happier to see someone leave. Hearing the door chime as the reporter and the photographer walked out filled him with relief.

He had done it. He had made it through the interviews and the picture-taking. After almost a year, he was going to be officially discharged from all the rehabilitation and therapy. Maybe everything had been on hold these past eleven months, but now he could pick up where he'd left off.

Charlie smiled at him, handing the file she'd been using to track his progress to Tracy, the receptionist. "Here's Mr. Buchanan's file. I think his discharge papers are on Leslie's desk. I'll run back and get them."

As Charlie left him in the doorway, retreating to Leslie's office in the back, he couldn't help wondering about the strained set of her jaw and mouth.

If he'd been anxious about being interviewed, she'd been downright uncomfortable. The entire time, she'd done everything she could to stay out of the way, keeping her head down, answering questions with the simplest responses. It probably hadn't been apparent to Rodriguez because she'd never met Charlie before, but to him, her behavior had been odd. Every other interaction he'd had with her, she'd been full of laughter, the center of the party. She had the kind of open smile that invited people to gather around her and that way of putting people at ease that had never come naturally to him. He could charm people, if he set his mind to, especially women, but that sort of natural charisma wasn't part of who he was.

Today? She'd been in hiding.

Still, her presence had made the entire experience much easier for him. How, he wasn't sure. He'd had a few other panic attacks over the past couple of months. The closer he got to boarding a plane and parachuting out, the worse they seemed to get. But the one before today had gone on much longer, been much worse. Something about Charlie's presence had calmed him. Maybe it was having someone there, because the other times he'd been alone. Or maybe it was something about Charlie specifically. He didn't know.

What he did know was that if she could do that today, maybe she could help him finish this up. He was going to get through rookie training. Every second for eleven months, he'd focused on that goal. He'd been derailed last year, but that wasn't going to happen this year. He'd pushed hard, physically. He was running again, lifting again. All of it. In a couple of weeks, if he stuck with the training regimen he'd devised, he'd be in top shape. Just like before.

But was he ready to jump? He wasn't sure. He'd been putting it off. He'd told himself he'd wait until he was physically fixed, until he was discharged. Except here he was, done with his rehab, and thinking about getting back in the air made his heartbeat kick up.

Charlie had helped, though. Somehow. He only needed to figure out how.

Sauntering over, he leaned against the doorjamb of Leslie's office and wiped sweat out of his eyes, on the shoulder of his T-shirt. "Hey, thanks for your help."

She didn't look up, digging under a mountain of papers. "You're welcome. I know the discharge papers are here. I'll have Tracy get your insurance paperwork together and we'll get you out of here."

"No, not with the therapy." He shrugged, crossing an arm over his chest and gripping his elbow, stretching out the shoulder he'd worked out. He'd pushed hard today, determined to prove to everyone that he was tip-top. Between the barometric pressure of the upcoming rain and his added effort, his recovered arm was sore. "I mean with what happened in here." He nudged his head toward Leslie's door.

"Oh." Charlie glanced up, pausing in her search, and offered him a smile. Something about it made him want to smile back. "No problem."

"No, really." He didn't like that she was waving her help off. "It would have been embarrassing to have that come out in the paper, that talking to a reporter made me panic."

"Well, talking to reporters would make me panic, too," she mumbled, her grin having faded. "Aha. Here are the forms." She lifted the paperwork, triumph on her face. She opened the drawer, and then started rooting around, a crinkle between her eyes.

"Can I help you find something?"

"I need a…pen…." The tip of her tongue peeked out the corner of her mouth in her concentration, and he found himself completely distracted by it. "There we go." She clicked the pen and started scribbling her initials in a few places, unaware that her full lips had derailed him.

Shaking his head, he crossed his arms over his chest. What the hell? He shouldn't be staring at her mouth. He definitely shouldn't notice how full and appealing the shape of it was. "Well, thank you for everything, seriously."

"No big deal." She tucked the page into a folder before holding it out to him. "There you go."

The phone on the desk beeped. "Miss Jones? One of your personal training clients is on the phone. Mr. Stephenson."

She leaned forward and pushed a button. "Thanks, Tracy. Tell Marcus I'll be with him in a moment."

"Personal training?"

"I do personal training on the side, through a local gym." She shrugged. "For extra cash. Anyway, tell Meg I said hey and that we need to get together for drinks. I'll text her this weekend."

"Will do." He could tell she was busy and wanted to dismiss him. She was working. But, irrationally, it bothered him that she wanted him to go. Because he wasn't as eager to leave her company. Why, he wasn't sure, and he refused to think too hard about it.

Besides, this was exactly the opportunity he needed. "Hey, do you have space for another client right now?"

She blinked up at him. Her eyes were a pretty brown, he noticed offhand, rimmed with thick lashes. "You're done with physical therapy."

"No, I mean as a personal training client." Not that he actually needed a trainer. He was fit and advanced enough that he could probably be a trainer himself. But hiring her would be the perfect excuse to spend more time with her. The way she'd helped him through his panic attack? If she had secret tips on how to do that, he needed to learn them.

He could probably ask, but if he did, he'd have to acknowledge that the attacks were more of an issue than he'd led her to believe. Not that they were, granted. A few bouts of anxiety weren't a problem. Once he got through a jump, he'd be fine. He was sure of it.

"You need a personal trainer?" She trailed her gaze over him, skeptical. And was that appreciation?

No. He was imagining that.

Thinking fast, he nodded. "It would be a big help. I'm supposed to start rookie training in a couple weeks." He left out that Mitch hadn't exactly cleared him yet. Need-to-know basis. "And I could use an extra push."

"You want me," she glanced down at herself, "to train you?"

Correction: "You want me"—she glanced down at herself—"to train you?" She waved her hand over him.

Fine, when she said it like that, he could see why she might wonder. Not that she wasn't in good shape. The workout gear she was wearing now, leggings and a tank top over a sports bra, revealed toned muscles, a flat belly, and shapely legs. Not that he had noticed before.

It's only that he was at least a foot taller than her petite frame. And, well, he'd already been training hard. He wouldn't brag, but he was all muscle right now.

"Not to point it out, Hunter, but you don't look like you need me. I usually work with people who are, I don't know, losing weight to take pressure off prior injuries. Or trying to get their blood sugar or cholesterol under control. Stuff like that. You?" Again, her eyes swept over him. Whatever was in that gaze made him want her to keep looking at him. "You don't need me."

She motioned to her phone. "I need to get this."

"Right." He didn't know how to convince her without sounding like a complete dick. "Thanks, though. I appreciated your help today."

She grinned, obviously thankful that he was dropping it. "Hey, no problem."

She nodded again. He backed away, and again, he couldn't figure out why he didn't really want to leave. He should be running out of here.

Snagging his gym bag, he slung it over his shoulder and headed toward the door. Her voice stopped him. "Hey, Hunter?"

"Yeah?"

She waved, this time her smile almost wistful. "Take care, okay?"

He waved back, swallowing around a surprisingly tight throat. What was going on here? "Will do, Charlie."

With nothing else to do, he left.

Chapter Four

"So Charlie does personal training, huh?" Hunter followed his sister into the kitchen of their mom's house the next night, depositing the dishes he'd gathered into the sink. He scraped the scraps into the garbage before rinsing the dishes and loading them in the dishwasher.

These family dinners had become more frequent this past year. They weren't always on the same day of the week thanks to everyone's erratic schedules, but they were nearly weekly.

His sister paused while putting leftovers into Tupperware to toss him a quizzical look. "My friend Charlie? Or is there a Charlie at the air center I don't know?"

"Your friend. Charlie."

"Oh. Yeah." She used the serving spoon to force the potatoes in before she sealed the lid. "Olivia works out with her. Says she's good."

"Yeah?"

"Yeah." She wrinkled her brow. "Why are you asking?" There was the skeptical sister routine.

"Well, I was thinking maybe she might be able to help me. You know, I need to hit it hard before training." That was true enough, if not the whole truth.

She washed her hands, drying them before reaching into her purse on the table to grab her phone. "Here, let me get her contact information."

"Actually, I was wondering if you could maybe ask her for me." He leaned back against the sink, playing it cool. Not because he didn't want to hang out with Charlie, but because Meg was his sister. There would be questions.

There were always questions.

"I think she'd be fine if you called. Here, let me send you her contact." Meg hadn't looked up from her phone.

Damn it. "It would be great if you could talk to her."

"Wait." She glanced up, phone in hand. Her eyes narrowed. "Why?"

He almost rolled his eyes. Questions, as predicted. None of his brothers was this wary. What was it about his sister that she had to question everything?

Then again, growing up with two older brothers and two younger brothers might be the reason she was so suspicious.

He sighed. "Because I already asked her."

"And?" Now her eyebrows were up.

"And she said no." He tried not to glare but probably failed.

"Huh." She locked her phone screen and slipped it into her back pocket, returning to the leftovers.

That didn't give him any answers. He glared at her auburn ponytail. "So, will you help me?"

"If she said no, then no. There have to be other trainers around. I can ask at my gym. I need to go run tonight anyway." She cast him a grin over her shoulder. "I'm on the downhill stretch of my training."

She was training for a marathon. Hunter didn't understand her fascination with running. He ran because he had to, for cardio and endurance. His weirdo sister thought it was fun. "After a full turkey dinner?"

"It's only a few miles."

"Right." At that, he did roll his eyes. Couldn't help it. "Listen, I'd rather it be her."

"Why?"

"Why?" he repeated.

"Yeah. Why?"

"Well." He didn't understand why it was this important that it was her. She'd helped him through his panic this morning. But he couldn't exactly tell Meg that. "Well, she's familiar with my recovery."

"She wasn't your physical therapist, right?"

"No," he hedged. "But she works there. She knows what Leslie did, I'm sure." He wasn't actually sure, but it was a good argument. "And, she's nice." Meg couldn't exactly refute that. Charlie was one of her friends. "She smiles a lot."

He had no idea why he'd added that. His sister must have wondered, too, because she gave him a look that said he was nuts. It was true, though. Charlie had an amazing smile. It made things better. Lighter, maybe. Like being in the sunshine.

He shook his head. Jesus. He wasn't this poetic.

"I think she's a good fit and I don't have time to test out someone else. I need to get going." True enough. Because the sooner he tackled whatever was going on and got jumping out of a plane again, the better.

"Seriously, I don't know why you can't call her yourself." Meg folded her arms over her chest, offering him a stubborn glare.

"Meg, honey, can't you see that your brother wants you to go to bat for him with a pretty girl?" Meg's boyfriend, Lance Roberts, carried a mostly empty casserole dish into the kitchen. "Look at him. He obviously needs help in the dating department. Who would want to go out with that guy?"

Hunter punched him in the arm, but he couldn't help grinning at the guy. When they were boys, they'd been the best of friends. After their fathers were killed jumping a wildfire and Lance's dad was blamed for the death of his and Meg's father, they'd grown apart—too much awfulness between them all. When Lance had returned last year to join the rookie training, everything had come out about what actually had transpired that day. In the end, Lance's father's name had been cleared and Hunter's uncle had killed himself, unable to deal with his own guilt, having set in motion the events that resulted in both men's deaths.

Since then, things had been better between him and Lance. It helped that Lance had saved Hunter's life, cutting the twisted parachute that would have interfered in his reserve parachute's deployment. If it hadn't been for Lance, Hunter would have died when his parachute hadn't opened. Instead, he'd been severely injured, barely escaping with his life.

Not that he'd been lucky. But he could acknowledge that it could have been worse.

That Lance clearly adored his sister didn't hurt his opinion of the guy either.

"Shut up, dickhead."

"Good comeback, asshole."

Hunter retaliated by throwing the towel at Lance's head. But his grin faded when he caught Meg's calculating stare. He wanted to deny that he was interested in Charlie. This wasn't about that. Sure, Charlie was attractive. Not exactly pretty in the conventional way, but she had nice eyes and a wide mouth. And her body, well, her body was smoking hot. She was shorter than he usually dated. He was a tall guy, so he usually dated taller girls. But something about her petite, strong, and compact body definitely did it for him.

Not that it was about that, either, though.

But he couldn't say that to Meg. Because whatever got her to call Charlie and convince her to help him would further his agenda.

Meg pulled her phone out of her pocket and tapped on the face for a second before slipping it back there and turning to the dishes again.

"Well?" he asked her. Seriously, sisters could be so annoying.

"I texted her. I'll see if she wants to get coffee or something tomorrow, after I run in the morning. It's Sunday, so she'll probably sleep in long enough for me to get some miles in."

He resisted the urge to fist pump, trying to play it cool, and ignored Lance's too-astute gaze. "Thanks, Meg. I owe you one."

* * * *

"So," Charlie started, sipping her smoothie. "What's this visit about?"

Though she always enjoyed getting together with Meg, the impromptu coffee talks and dessert breaks had been few and far between these past few months. Meg had been working longer hours, trying to bank her time so that when she cut back to start rookie training again, it wouldn't impact her checkbook. But, more, she was spending a lot of time with Lance.

Which was what Charlie suspected this early Sunday smoothie run was really about. Meg and Lance had been together for almost a year. She wondered if they were ready to take the next step.

She hoped so. She liked Lance, but mostly she loved how happy her friend was. Meg deserved all the best in the world.

"What? I need a special reason to come hang out with my friend?"

"Early on a Sunday? Yes," Charlie deadpanned. When Meg laughed, Charlie lowered her smoothie. Banana and peanut butter. One of her favorites. "Seriously, though. You didn't drive up here on a weekend just to get breakfast with me."

They were sitting outside the smoothie shop, enjoying the unseasonably warm weather. The spring could be fickle like this, offering warmth one day and then changing its mind and snowing the next. Part of the beauty of Oregon.

"I came up to run. Three weeks until my marathon."

"Way to go." Charlie lifted her cup in salute. "How's it going?"

"Good." Meg leveled her with a serious gaze. "But you're right. This is about Hunter."

That was not what she'd been expecting her to say. "Your brother?"

"How many Hunters do you know?"

Charlie waved with her drink. "Right. Of course."

"He asked me to ask you to help him train." Meg continued to study her as she took another sip.

Internally, Charlie groaned. Of all the things she'd hoped to talk with her friend about today, this wasn't one of them.

Not that she hadn't considered Hunter's proposal repeatedly over the past two days. Since he'd left her office on Friday, her thoughts had strayed to him more than a few times. How they'd seemed to connect over his panic attack, a sort of "us against the reporter" teamwork thing. How many times she'd been uncomfortably aware of him, his big, sweaty, gorgeous body. How much she'd wanted to agree to be his personal trainer, even though working with someone she found attractive would be difficult.

"Did he tell you I already turned him down?"

"He did. But he wanted me to see if I could change your mind." Meg grinned, shifting out of the sunlight and further under the umbrella. With her fair skin and red hair, Meg burned easily.

"Meg…"

"If you're too busy, have too many other clients, I'll tell him that. No biggie. I just wanted to let you know that he was excited to work with you."

"Why?" Seriously, this was the question that had rattled around in her head over and over. "He is clearly in amazing shape. Why would he pick me to train him? I'm pretty sure there's nothing I can teach him." He was so cut and physically fit, there was probably stuff he could teach *her*.

Meg's gaze trailed over Charlie's shoulder, as if she'd become lost in her own thoughts. Charlie watched her closely. Since her conversation with Hunter, she couldn't shake the concern that she'd left her friend too much to herself. After everything had happened last year, she'd probably needed someone to talk to. She had Lance, and she'd told Charlie that her relationship with her mom had improved. But Meg was her friend. She should have checked on her.

"How did things go with him, on Friday?" Meg finally asked.

"Fine. I mean, it was fine, I think. Why, did he say something?" The words were fast, breathy, and immediately Charlie regretted them. What was more suspicious than an overly fast denial?

"Nothing, really." Her friend's eyes narrowed. "Do you like him?"

Oh God. Determined to deflect, she tried to laugh. It sounded forced. "Of course I like him. He's your brother. What's not to like?"

"You're avoiding me."

This was the problem with good friends. They knew you too well. "Fine. I think he's mildly attractive."

Meg's eyebrows shot up. "Yeah?"

"Oh, shut up. Fine. Really attractive. He might be your brother, but even an objective bystander could see that he's incredibly good-looking." This was going all wrong. She sighed. "That's why I can't train him."

"I think you can."

Charlie set her empty smoothie container on the table. "Didn't you hear me? I'm attracted to your brother." She enunciated each word. As if this wasn't embarrassing enough.

"Yeah, I heard you. But he wants you to train him. That he asked is interesting. He hasn't reached out for help from anyone, not since everything happened."

"That can't be right." There was no way someone with as much family and as many friends as Hunter, someone as good-looking and talented... There was no way they wouldn't be surrounded by people who wanted to help them.

"I've tried." Meg shook her head. "I tried to get him to talk. Lance has made a lot of headway with him, regaining their friendship. But Hunter had been incredibly close with Will. Losing that friendship hit him hard." Will, Meg and Hunter's oldest brother, had been the one who'd sabotaged the parachute, assuming Lance would use it. Instead, Hunter had worn the twisted chute and nearly been killed.

"I mean, I don't know what I can do." If his family couldn't get through, what could they expect from her, someone who was barely even a friend?

"No, I get it. I was just happy." Meg sighed. "To hear he'd reached out. That's good news. Maybe that means he's ready to open up to all of us."

Charlie watched her friend's face, the hope there making her ache for her, for her brother, maybe for all of them.

She wanted to be part of that recovery for all of them. But she couldn't take on that kind of responsibility, not when she could barely get herself together.

The interview that she'd helped Hunter get through last week had been published in today's paper, and the worst had happened. It had included a picture of her and him, working through their exercises. Her face had been turned slightly, not giving the camera a direct view of her features. But it was enough.

It had been years. Joshua must recognize that she hadn't been the only cause of his incarceration.

She could hope, but the possibility that she might have a psycho breathing down her neck at any moment had ravaged her nerves.

Surely that was a sign that she wasn't in any place to help anyone. Especially not the hot, talented, interesting brother of one of her closest friends.

"I am sure I know someone who could use some extra money," she finally offered. Even as she said the words, she balked. *She* could use the extra money. After living here for a few years, she'd begun to wonder if maybe she could settle down in Oregon. Set down roots and start her own physical therapy practice. She'd watched Leslie and her partner run Myers and Long, learned so much about the business of it from them.

She could do it, if she could find the capital to begin. That's why she'd been taking on personal training clients. The money was great, especially because she worked out, too. It killed two birds with one stone: she stayed in shape and she dropped the extra cash in her "Future Business Fund."

Three weeks of extensive physical training would be a pretty decent bump to her bottom line. It hurt to turn it down.

Meg shrugged. "If you're sure."

"I'm not." She sighed as Meg laughed. "*I* could use the money. I'm getting close to the number that the business loan guy told me I needed to hit."

"To start your own place?" Meg's eyes lit up. "That's awesome."

"I said close. I'm not there."

"Listen, Charlie, why don't you give Hunter a chance? Work out with him a couple times. If it doesn't work, no harm done. You could use the cash and he needs to be ready for training. If he gets there and fails again…" She shook her head. "I'm not sure what he'll do."

Charlie's chest tightened. Was that even a possibility? Her mind strayed to Hunter, to his toned physique. He was in amazing shape. But maybe Meg meant from a confidence perspective. It must have been difficult, to face training again after having a year to remember what had happened last time.

"I don't know—"

"Come on. One day." Meg grinned. Obviously she could see Charlie was weakening.

She raised her hands in defeat. "One day. But let him know that I'm not sure this is going to work out. That I'm busy or whatever. We'll see how it goes. No promises."

But Meg already had her phone out, texting.

Chapter Five

I'm not guaranteeing anything. Charlie texted like she did everything else: straightforward. The words made Hunter grin.

No expectations, he shot back. It was true. He didn't expect her to do anything for him physically, but he couldn't deny that she settled him.

He folded his pillow in half, tucking it under his head. It was Sunday night, and Meg had told him earlier that Charlie had agreed to help. Wanting to connect and make plans before she had a chance to change her mind, he'd shot Charlie a text and thanked her for taking him on.

This had been her response.

Chuckling, he watched as the three dots appeared, signaling that she was typing.

Good, because I'm not sure how I'll help, but I'll take your money.

He laughed at that. *Fine with me.*

She hadn't even waited for his response as she kept typing. *I'm sure you run faster, jump higher, lift more, etc. than I do.*

No doubt. But that wasn't the point. *I need moral support and someone to whip me into shape. I'll do the heavy lifting.*

What did you have in mind?

What *did* he have in mind for her?

Despite his intention to remain platonic, his brain supplied him with a barrage of images of her petite frame with her slim hips and high breasts.

Damn it. That wasn't what this was about. He needed to stay on task.

She was right; he didn't need her to help him lift more or run faster. He had a pretty good handle on that stuff. What he needed was morale-based training. Except he didn't know how to ask for that.

He must have been taking too long to answer, because she prodded, *A run in the morning? I usually go at six.*

Biting the inside of his lip, he inhaled. Well, here went nothing.

I actually ran a bunch today. I was going to bungee tomorrow. You wanna come?

She didn't immediately respond. The lack of three dots had his heart picking up. That sounded an awful lot like he was asking her out on a date. Which he wasn't. This wasn't a romantic thing. This was him, wanting to hire her because she pacified the panicky monster inside him.

Not a date. Then again, when he phrased it like that, it didn't sound any better.

Finally, she responded. *Bungee jumping?*

He typed fast. *Yeah, haven't been in a while. Wanna come? Our first training session.*

There. That sounded almost like he didn't care, even as his heart was racing. After a pause, he added, *I get it if you don't.*

There were no dots for a long time. Finally, he lowered the phone, resting it against his chest after the screen darkened. He'd been holding it too close to his face, as if he could physically will her to respond if he stared hard enough.

This had been a mistake. He should have left this alone.

The phone chimed.

Sure.

The intensity of his relief frightened him. Had he been that invested in whether she agreed?

He rubbed his chin, staring at that short reply. If he was, then he needed to get a grip. This was about her doing him a favor, even if she would have no idea she was doing it. She would "train" him and unwittingly help him get over whatever was causing these stupid panic attacks.

He was no doctor or psychologist, but he guessed the attacks had something to do with him dreading parachuting again. Even thinking about it made his palms slick. But facing a jump with Charlie there somehow it didn't seem as scary. She was so calm. Steady. Like she understood how fear worked.

It didn't make sense, but he didn't care. If having her around helped, he'd pay to have her around.

Have you been before?

No.

A novice. He had no idea if that was good or bad. As long as she came, that's all that mattered. *Can you go in the morning?*

I need to be at work by 11.
Meet me at 8.
Ugh. Bring coffee.
He laughed. Not a morning person. Noted. But the last thing he wanted was her jumping on a full stomach. *I'll take you to breakfast afterward.*

She didn't respond, so he shot off the address of the jumping bridge.

When he stuck the phone on his nightstand to charge, the smile faded. Was he using her? He shifted to his side, punching his pillow. It wasn't as if he wasn't going to pay her to train him. In fact, when she'd mentioned her rate, he'd offered higher, insisting it was on short notice. She didn't argue. She would be compensated. Still, it might not be fair that he wasn't being truthful.

Honestly, though, how would she know? He was a master at keeping his thoughts to himself, even from his closest friends and family. No one needed the workings of his mind. So she helped him through something in his mental space while she was helping him out with physical training. Two for one.

As long as he kept reminding himself that she was his sister's friend and she was unknowingly doing him this favor. He'd keep it light, professional.

And he'd keep his hands off.

* * * *

"You said nothing about me jumping." Maybe Charlie should have read that between the lines. It had been late last night when they were texting. She had been in her jammies, her bra off and her hair in a clip, watching *Grey's Anatomy* reruns. Apparently, she had read this situation all wrong. "You said you were going bungee-jumping, asked if I wanted to come along. Not that you wanted to me to jump, too."

She had assumed they'd work out afterward. That wherever he was taking her had some sort of workout situation.

Instead, they stood on an insanely high bridge. Hunter held a clipboard with paperwork on it, signing and initialing in a bunch of spots. Waivers, she guessed. In case he died.

Jesus.

He tossed her a teasing grin. "Come on, Charlie girl. You mean you've never been tempted to jump off something high?"

That wasn't the point. Sure, she had those same weird urges everyone had when they were up high—to throw herself out into the open, to experience that free-falling rush. It sounded terrifying and exhilarating and completely crazy.

She was rational enough to ignore those urges.

Because jumping off tall things was nuts. Below her, she had no idea how wide the stream was that ran through the canyon. Even from this high, though, she could tell that the rocks down there were sharp enough to mangle her. Call her vain, but she preferred her body the way it was right now. Unmangled.

He must have followed her line of sight. "You don't get that close to the ground."

She pointed at the cord. "That is a lot of line."

The outfitter from the bungee-jumping company must have seen her doubts, because he launched into an entire description of how it worked, pointing out all of their safety precautions. Charlie listened at half-attention, her eyes on the platform that stuck out over the bridge's lip.

When the guy picked up the full body harness, she lifted her eyes to Hunter. "Yeah, no."

He laughed. "Come on. Carpe diem." Except his smile faded as he stared at the harness, too. The expression that replaced it was inscrutable. Determination? Maybe. He'd said he hadn't done this stuff in a while. Maybe this was him, getting back into it.

Carpe diem.

The phrase struck her in the stomach, right where she stored how much she missed her parents.

The last she'd heard from them, they were in New Mexico, learning to make pottery from some artisan. Before that, they'd spent the last summer in Kansas in Tornado Alley, experiencing the "exhilaration of Mother Nature's destruction." The year before it had been Maine, for fishing. They didn't have cell phones, so she usually had to wait until they found their way to a landline they could call her from. Or when they remembered.

As a young child, she'd figured that everyone moved a couple of times a year. They'd lived in strange places—rented trailers, tents, hotel rooms. Her parents would pick up odd jobs. Usually her mom cleaned houses and her father did lawn work. They didn't have much money, but that never seemed to stress them out. They were as devoted to each other now as they had been when she was small.

They always said that. Carpe diem. Seize the day.

God, she missed them. She needed to give them a call.

"You know what, Charlie," Hunter offered. "No sweat. I'll do my jump and then I'll take you to breakfast before work." He winked, then glanced down at the guy who would help him into his harness and do his safety check. "I'll do it." She held her hand out to the guy with the waivers.

"What?" The grin was gone from Hunter's face.

"I'll do it. I'll bungee-jump." How scary could it be? Lots of people did it and lived.

"I was teasing you." Now his forehead was crinkled like he was convinced she was crazy. Like this had been her idea. "I'm sorry, but you don't—"

"No, I want to." She clicked the pen open and started filling out her information. "Seize the day, right?"

"Yeah, but you know, maybe you should start carpe diem-ing with something else. Like, try a new coffee flavor." He stepped around the guy helping him and placed his hands on her shoulders. Meeting her eyes, he squeezed. "Seriously. I figured that you'd have the night to change your mind, if you wanted to. This isn't something to decide on the spur of the moment."

"I'm doing it." He didn't know her well yet, but when he did, he'd realize that she'd made up her mind.

Go where life blew you. That's what her parents always said.

Something in his eyes shifted. He'd teased her earlier, but she got the impression he wasn't as gung ho about doing this jump as he let on. Almost as if he was using her refusal to distract himself.

But why would he pretend?

His uncertainty hardened her resolve. "I'll go first."

The outfitter's smile widened. "Savage." He walked her through the waivers, and she paid close attention, making sure she understood everything—the risks and the harness. This particular company used a full body harness to avoid strain on the ankles and knees. Apparently, it allowed her to do flips in the air, too.

Picturing herself somersaulting in the air made her grin.

After the safety waivers were taken care of, an instructor went over the best way to jump.

A swallow dive.

They expected her to throw herself off the edge of the bridge, her arms outstretched and her feet together like some Olympic diver.

Even as she acknowledged how bizarre that was, the joy bubbled inside her. She laughed with it, the exhilaration of what she was about to do pumping through her. It had been a long time since she'd done something out of the ordinary, reckless even.

"When you finish deceleration, the boat at the bottom will retrieve you." The instructor finished checking all of her gear once more. "So we don't have to pull you all the way back up."

"Does seem counterproductive, after I go to all the trouble to get down there."

He laughed. "Right. You're good to go." Stepping back, he motioned toward the ledge, ten meters or so away.

She stared at it and the open air in front of her.

Hunter's hand on her sleeve stopped her. "You don't have to do this."

Scanning his face, she figured out exactly what mixed with the determination in his eyes: stark terror.

"You've done this before, right?" She kept her voice calm, steady. There might be a heady mix of excitement and fear coursing through her, but it was life affirming. Whatever was happening with Hunter, though, wasn't giving him that same high, and she wanted it to. She wanted to share the glorious headiness of this experience. So she held his gaze and focused on him. "I bet you've done this hundreds of times."

"Not hundreds," he admitted. "But dozens, yeah." He ducked his head and shrugged, and the entire gesture tugged at her heart. He might have done this before, but she would bet that his present anxiety was a new element to the jumping—and right now, she'd do whatever it took to make him feel better.

Even pretend she was totally cool with jumping off a bridge.

"So this is no sweat for you." She made the declaration as if it were factual, even though this jump didn't seem easy for him. "And if you can do it, so can I."

"I haven't..." He shook his head. "Not since the...fall. I haven't."

Charlie stilled. Why hadn't this occurred to her before? His accident had been caused by a twisted parachute and his inability to get his spare to open. She couldn't imagine what those moments had felt like, free-falling, helpless because his gear had failed. No wonder he wasn't too eager to jump now.

Studying his face, she could still see it, though, in the steely set of his jaw: determination. He had come here to do this jump, to tough through it.

She lowered her voice so the instructor wouldn't overhear her. "That's why you came today. So you could get over that."

He nodded curtly, swallowing hard.

That made sense. But if he was hell-bent on doing the jump, why was he suddenly trying to convince her not to?

As his fingers tightened further on her arm, the pieces came together. "You're afraid for me."

There was no other option. He was worried about her.

They barely knew each other. Nothing in the times they'd hung out gave her any indication that he liked her at all. Yet here he was, worrying. That it came from his own fears since his accident tugged at her heart in a way that was dangerous.

She smiled at him, squeezing his arm again before stepping away. No way was she backing out now. "You'll have to come down, then. Make sure I'm okay."

Without another word, she joined the instructor, who went through one more safety check before giving her a thumbs-up.

She glanced at Hunter once more, finding his gaze inscrutable. She blew him a kiss.

And then she jumped.

Chapter Six

He didn't breathe correctly until she was in the boat.

Hunter paced along the platform, his hands on his hips and his heart pounding so fast he was afraid he'd give himself cardiac trouble. It was almost like a panic attack, but worse because it wasn't about him.

It was about Charlie.

As she had stood at the ledge, his mind had offered image after image of horror. They all included blood and gore, each one worse than the last. He had to force himself not to reach for her, to pull her away from that ledge.

Visions from his own fall mixed in with his macabre imagination, painting his own horrifying experience over Charlie's face.

Except, nothing like that happened. She screamed as she jumped, yelling her face off. He wasn't sure, but he might have caught a couple of *woo-hoo*s in there.

When she'd stood there, staring at him, she'd been solid. He'd seen a lot of things in his life. He'd been a hotshot, facing wildfires that sometimes seemed to rage like the flames of hell. In the face of them, he'd been awestruck and afraid, almost equally. He'd watched men skydive and parachute. None of them had ever looked as contained as she did. Sure, there had been excitement and that nervous-fear buzz about her.

The core of Charlie was as strong as steel.

As she'd smiled at him before she jumped, he got the impression she was telling him something. Don't be afraid, maybe. Or *you got this*.

All strapped into his harness, he glanced over the rail. Below, he could barely make her out, only the speck of her orange T-shirt.

Did she have fun? Did she hate it, wish he'd never suggested this? Wish he'd never dragged her into his messed-up plans in the first place? Think she'd be better off if he left her alone and stepped out of her life forever?

He wasn't going to know unless he got down there and asked her.

"I'm ready," he told the instructor. Was he? Who knew, but he wasn't going to let himself stand there trapped in his own skull any longer. Time to face this head-on.

You'll have to come down, then. Make sure I'm okay.

Stepping to the ledge, he focused on that, on getting to the bottom and checking on Charlie. His heart pounding, he swallowed to keep the bile from rising in his mouth. Closing his eyes, he jumped.

The rush was immediate. The dipping in his stomach, the flash of panic and exhilaration. He couldn't help it; he opened his eyes, absorbing the sights around him.

And then there it was, taking him over, singing through him with a sweetness his body remembered but his mind had completely blocked. The peace. He'd forgotten all about that, the silence as he fell, the pureness of feeling at one with the air around him.

As the water rushed toward him, he had no idea if he'd been screaming the entire time, but he definitely was now as he decelerated at the end of the jump line.

The initial terror gone, he enjoyed the rest of his jump, even managing a few flips and twists, laughing the entire time.

When they unhooked him on the boat, he folded Charlie into a hug, laughing. The lightness, as if a huge weight had been lifted off of him, made him want to shout, to dance. He'd done it. He'd managed his first free fall since nearly dying.

If he could do this, maybe everything was going to be all right. Until he had stood on that ledge, he hadn't realized how much he'd questioned his ability to get back up there, to parachute again. And if he couldn't parachute, how would he get through smokejumper training?

But the bungee jump gave him hope. Maybe he could pick up with the rest of his life and pretend the last year of hellish rehab and mental uncertainty had never happened.

Charlie held on to him, and they did a sort of hug and jump combo, full of laughing and talking over each other.

"Did you see me?" she asked, her cheeks pink and her eyes shining. "I jumped off a bridge!"

"Yeah, you did. And screamed like you were on fire." He laughed, but he couldn't help noticing how well she wore exhilaration. As he held her, he also noticed how well she fit against him. Charlie was petite and rounded in exactly the right spots. And with her dark, windblown curls and the excitement on her face, she was the most gorgeous thing he'd ever seen.

The air between them charged, and she stilled, shifting slightly away. But the smile remained on her face. "Yeah, well, you sounded like you were being murdered. I'm sure I was better than that."

The additional space gave him much-needed perspective. What was he thinking? He'd told himself he would keep his distance from her, at least *this* kind of distance. Meg had made it clear that Charlie wasn't interested in anything more than training.

He needed her to help him get past whatever mental constipation he was having about jumping.

She'd already helped, if today's success was any indication. The least he could do was keep it professional. And stop noticing how great she made him feel and how gorgeous she looked.

As the boat took off toward the parking lot where a truck would return them to their cars, Charlie chattered about how exciting the jump had been and how much fun she'd had.

"So, when are you going to go again?" she asked, as they arrived at their cars.

"We just finished," he said, laughing. But he didn't have an answer. Was that a one-and-done reprieve? Was his hope that things were fine now misplaced? What if this entire exercise was a fluke, and the next time he got into the sky he'd be a bag of nerves again?

He shook his head, determined to leave those worries in the future. Right now, he needed to bask in this win. "Let me buy you breakfast?"

"Sold. I know just the place."

* * * *

"I'm picking it up." Hunter covered the check with his hand. The cashier, Emily, glanced at Charlie, wiggling her eyebrows with a quick grin before she turned to the next order. Charlie scowled after her. Since she came to this café all the time—it was three doors down from her office—the cashier knew her well enough to know she didn't regularly share breakfast with hot guys.

Charlie rolled her eyes at him. "It's smoothies. And a muffin."

"I'm still covering it." He swiped the receipt off the table, reaching for his wallet. "It's the least I can do."

"For what?" She rolled her eyes. "You're already paying me to train you. So far, all I did was jump off a bridge. Not sure I'm being very helpful."

He laughed but didn't respond, only inserted his card into the payment pad and pushed a few buttons.

She'd brought up going for a run again when they had gotten to the smoothie place. He waved her off, telling her they could run tomorrow. When she pressed him for a time, he evaded: told her he had a meeting in the morning, something about lunch with his mom, and trailed off.

So he didn't want her for running, something she was actually good at, but he did want her to go bungee jumping with him. Something she'd never done before.

It didn't make sense.

As he held the door for her, stepping out of the smoothie shop, she paused on the sidewalk. "Seriously, Hunter. I don't know that I helped at all." She inhaled. "I almost feel bad taking any payment."

He shook his head. "Absolutely not. This was incredibly helpful. I mean it."

Inexplicably, she believed him. When they'd been standing on the ledge, she had wondered if he might not go through with the jump. Which was strange, because it had been his idea. Even when she was at the bottom, in the boat, she'd figured there was a good chance he might balk.

When he joined her, she'd been exhilarated, the remains of the adrenaline flooding her, causing her to ramble on. Now that she looked back, she didn't think he'd been that happy. He'd only seemed relieved.

As she studied his face, she tried to figure out what she was missing. He'd needed to get back to jumping. But she couldn't shake the impression that there was more to it than that. There was something he wasn't telling her.

Finally, she shrugged. "Hey, fine with me. It's your money."

"Yes it is." He chuckled.

Then his hand found the small of her back, and her concerns fled. The warmth of his fingers there settled her, anchoring her in her body somehow.

Absolutely not. Attaching any sort of warm fuzzies to Hunter Buchanan was strictly against the rules. Not only was she his trainer, but he was her friend's brother. Meg was important to her. She didn't have a lot of friends, so she wasn't about to mess things up with one of the few she did have.

And mess things up was what she did. She'd chosen so badly the last time that she'd needed to skip town, stay in hiding.

That could not happen this time. So whatever strange wave of contentment and gooey feeling was going through her mind, she needed to nip that in the bud hard.

"I need your money." A new voice cut into the confusion that had been swirling through her. It came from behind her, so she didn't even see the girl who spoke at first. But Hunter must have, because he stiffened, shifting so fast she hardly saw him.

Standing on her tiptoes, she glanced around Hunter's arm. "What's going on?"

Only then did she see the gun. The woman holding it was emaciated, and her arm shook with the exertion it took to wield the weapon. She kept glancing around with wide eyes, vibrating with nervous energy. Her hair was disheveled, her cheeks sunken and gaunt.

A drug addict.

"You have the money. I need it." The woman shifted her weight, waving the weapon. "You have to give it to me. Now."

"We don't have any money." Hunter's voice was calm, low, but he pushed Charlie back and behind him, away from the weapon.

"No." The woman's voice bordered on hysteria. "You're lying. He told me she had the money. That I needed to get it from her. I need it." By the end of this tirade, her arm was shaking and she was screaming. Luckily, her increased volume came with additional scrutiny. Yelling permeated the fear coursing through Charlie, and she vaguely registered movement, running maybe. The other patrons must be figuring out what was going on. She wasn't sure, though. There was a gun. Someone was pointing a gun at her. It was sleek, black, and large in the woman's small hands. After all these years of hiding and playing it safe, everything had caught up with her.

"I need it. The money." The woman advanced toward them, and Hunter shifted her, stepping back so quickly that he almost tripped her.

"Put the gun down!" The shout came from the opposite direction, across the street. "Get down, now!"

Sweet Lord, it was a cop. Charlie's relief was so intense she almost crumbled under it. She shouldn't be surprised. They were in downtown Bend, and the hospital wasn't more than a few blocks away. Surely there would be police officers around.

"She has my money!" the woman yelled, pointing the gun in the air.

When it fired, the recoil surprised the woman, making her drop the gun on the ground. As she fell to her knees, crying, the police officer stormed forward, bringing her to the ground and whipping some handcuffs on her. Even as the policewoman restrained her, the addict struggled, her wild eyes on Charlie.

The entire time, she was screaming. "She has my money. She has it. I need it."

Hunter's arms enfolded Charlie, and only then did she realize she was quaking. She was thankful when he tightened his grip, holding her up. "I got you."

The next minutes were a blur. The policewoman had called for backup, and it arrived almost immediately. Or maybe it didn't. It could have taken longer. Charlie couldn't tell through her disorientation.

Hunter sat her down at one of the outside tables at the smoothie shop. A cop asked her questions, but she didn't start to feel more herself until Hunter pressed a cup of coffee in her hands. She sipped, and it warmed her.

"Did you know that woman?" Another cop sat next to her while a paramedic looked her over. When he stood, nodding at the policeman, he confirmed what she already knew: physically, she was fine.

Physically.

She shook her head. "No." She glanced to where Hunter paced. He ran his hands over his hair. "You should check him out, too. This was scary for both of us." He'd stood between her and a woman with a pistol. Surely he was disconcerted.

He paused his pacing to offer her a half grin. "I'm okay, Char."

"You're sure?" She narrowed her eyes on him.

The police officer interrupted them. "Miss Jones. You said you don't know her."

She forced herself to focus on the cop. "Yes. I mean, that's correct. I don't know her."

The officer glanced between her and Hunter. "What did she say?"

"She kept going on and on about how I had her money." Charlie didn't understand what that meant. She wasn't even carrying cash. She'd stuck her credit card in the pouch she'd attached to her phone case. "She isn't well. Is she high? Medicated?"

"Meth," Hunter offered.

During her schooling, she'd learned about methamphetamines. How they caused a lot of physical damage. How addicts would spend the rest of their addicted life craving that first, perfect high. How paranoid and erratic they could act. She'd never come across one before, though.

"Maybe that's it, then. Maybe she thinks I'm someone else." She swung her gaze between them, seeking reassurance. "If she was tweaking, she might have confused me with someone she knew, someone who owed her money or something." Across the street, they were loading her into a police car and medics were checking her. She was flailing, obviously in distress. "Will they be able to ask her? When she calms down?"

The policeman closed his notepad, tucking it in his pocket, his mouth thin. "Don't know. Maybe." He sighed, and it was the sound of someone who had seen and heard too much. "Hey, if you want a ride to the hospital, I can drive you."

"I'm fine," she said firmly. All she wanted was to forget all about this.

"Me too." Hunter offered his hand. "Thank you, though."

After the policeman walked away, Hunter leaned over, studying her. "Are you sure you're okay?"

She wasn't. But what she was sure of was that she didn't want to go to the hospital, and she definitely didn't want to spend any more time answering questions about why this girl might have targeted her.

Was there a chance that this had something to do with Joshua? Had he found her? Sending a meth addict with a gun to rob her didn't make any sense. Joshua had always been more hands-on than that.

Much more hands-on.

No, it was probably a fluke. She'd read recently that the opioid and methamphetamine market scourge had increased in their county in recent months.

Would there ever come a day when she didn't automatically think everything had to do with Joshua? He'd been in jail when she had left Chicago. Someday she'd need to stop looking over her shoulder. Today wasn't that day, though.

"Yeah, I'm okay. We just must have been in the wrong place at the wrong time." She stood, wiping her hands on her legs. She could see the front door of her office, could see Tracy standing in the door, scanning the scene, trying to see what was going on. The building beckoned to her, safe and predictable. Everything that had happened pressed down on her, and she suddenly needed to get out of there. "Listen, I'm going to be late for work. Thanks for the smoothie, and for everything." As she stared up at him, she remembered how he'd put himself between her and a crazed drug addict with a gun. A "thank you" didn't seem to cover something like that.

He shrugged, tapping the table beside him. "No problem."

"Um, did you want to train together tomorrow, then?" God, what an awkward transition. She couldn't possibly be this socially inept.

Glancing around, he shifted his weight and shrugged again. "Not tomorrow. After my morning appointment and lunch with Mom, I promised Dak and Lance that I'd hang out with them. We were going to hike with packs."

He was going hiking tomorrow? Once again she wondered why he was paying her if he was doing so much of the heavy training with others.

"How about a run the day after, though?" he asked quickly, as if he were reading her mind. "You have clients in the morning, right?" When she nodded, he continued. "We can go after you're done."

"Sure." She shrugged. Whatever. It was a loss to his pocketbook, not hers. "Sounds good. After lunch then." She edged closer to her office door.

"Okay, Charlie girl." His eyes narrowed. "You're really okay?"

"Definitely," she said, too quickly, taking a few more steps.

He watched as she backed away. "All right, then. I'll text you tomorrow."

As she spun and hurried to her office, she wished she wasn't looking forward to talking to him again quite as much.

* * * *

"So she just went to work after that?" Lance asked as he rubbed a hand towel over his face.

"Yeah. The police asked her some questions, she told them she never saw the girl before, and that was it." Hunter wiped the sweat out of his eyes, blinking through the salty sting. He'd finished his run with Lance and his smokejumper friends. Seven miles through rocky and hilly terrain. He was pleased that he didn't have any trouble keeping up with them. Another sign that he was ready to start training.

Now, he stood at the bottom of the trail with Lance and their friend Dak. Though the afternoon Oregon sun was bright, a cool breeze chilled the moisture from his workout.

"Did you believe her?" He shouldn't be surprised that Dak was skeptical. He'd never met Charlie.

"Absolutely." And he did. She had been as surprised as he had. "Besides, she's not the sort to lie well."

"Agreed." As Meg's boyfriend, Lance had spent enough time with her to know her well, too.

Did he know her well? Hunter wasn't sure. He felt like he did. There was something between them, something he couldn't deny.

When the armed woman had come at them, his first inclination had been to put himself between Charlie and the gun. He considered himself a regular guy, the kind of guy who would be a hero, if he was put in the right circumstances. His parents had raised him right. He'd even chosen a job that helped people regularly. He'd pulled people from burning buildings, helped them afterward if they were hurt. He never hesitated. But he'd never experienced the intense need to protect someone before, not the way he'd felt when he'd seen Charlie in danger.

There was a connection between them. Whatever it was, he knew her, deep down. He was sure of it.

And he was certain she wasn't a good liar. "Besides, I agree with her. I think it must have been random."

"Could be. There's lots of meth around right now." Dak shrugged out of his sweaty T-shirt, tossed it into the back of his truck, and yanked his gym bag off the front seat. "Heidi said they're finding pop-up shops all through the national forests. Forest Services is having a hard time keeping up with all the cleanup." For the past decade or so, cooks had been moving their meth labs out of the city and into rural areas to avoid police scrutiny. The stuff could be cooked anywhere, and because the national forests in Oregon were so vast and relatively close to the cities, they were prime locations. The risks the labs posed—as fire hazards and sites of toxic materials—had elevated them as a major problem for the Forest Services.

"Not to mention Johnny Santillo is back in the business." Sledge, one of the other smokejumpers who worked with Dak and Lance in Redmond, joined them at Dak's truck. When Hunter had met Dak and Lance at the air center for their hike, the guy had offered to go with them. Though he'd never liked the guy, Hunter had been a hotshot with him in Redmond. There hadn't been an easy way to say no without looking like a complete asshole. According to Dak and Lance, though, Sledge had come a long way since training, and he trusted their opinions. "He got out of jail a few months ago."

"What?" Hunter put his hands on his hips. "That guy was supposed to be put away for at least another five."

Sledge shrugged. "Good behavior, they said." He snorted. "But I'll bet it had less to do with good behavior and more to do with great connections."

"You think he knew someone on the parole board?"

"Paid someone, you mean?" Sledge smirked. "Yeah. That's what I mean."

Sledge was a lot of things—a meticulous perfectionist, kind of arrogant, bit of a pain in the ass—but he wasn't a liar. And he knew people, people who would tell him stuff like that.

"Shit."

"Yeah."

When they were hotshots, they'd stumbled on a meth lab while they'd been working a wildfire. The two cooks inside had been kids, neither more than sixteen. Due to their inexperience, the cooks had accidentally blown the place up, but when they'd called their boss, the distributor and financier of the drugs, he'd refused to help, leaving them stranded in the woods. They'd been nearly starved to death by the time the hotshots arrived.

In the days that followed, the cooks had refused to talk to the police, but Hunter had worked with them. They reminded him of his younger twin brothers—and while they had made some bad decisions, he didn't think they should take the fall for someone else's drug operation. Finally, after some coaxing, they described the entire network of meth labs all run by one man—Johnny Santillo—with cooks living in similar situations across the national forests. When it came time to testify against him, they did.

"No wonder Heidi's seeing more meth again." Hunter shook his head. "That guy is bad news."

"Not just Heidi. The cops I know in Redmond and Bend, too." Sledge rubbed his wet hair. "Santillo might not be the only meth dealer in town, but he's one of the biggest. And he's only been gone for a couple of years. Not long enough for his network to disintegrate."

Well then, maybe Heidi was right. Maybe running into this addict on the street had been coincidence.

Apparently it had meant a lot to Charlie, to make sure that it was a coincidence, that the cop agreed with her assessment. Then again, in stressful situations, everyone wanted to make sense of why things happened to them.

He could relate.

"We already had some training this spring about what to do if we run across a meth lab when we're out on a fire. Pretty much stay away from it, that was my takeaway." Lance tossed his gym bag into the back of his Jeep. Shrugging, he closed the back window. "Nasty messes."

"Yeah." Nasty and dangerous.

"Hey, stiffs," Sledge called from next to his car. "I'm done gossiping. I don't stay the best with just hiking. I'm off to the gym. Later." He didn't wait for them to say goodbye, sliding into the front seat and driving off.

"You know." Dak rubbed the back of his head, watching him go. "Sometimes I think he's getting better and other times I think he's still just a giant douche."

Hunter laughed, opening the door on his beat-up TrailBlazer.

"So we'll see you next week? At training?" Lance's question was light and offhand, as if he was asking if Hunter planned to join them at the bar for drinks or something. But Hunter could hear the seriousness in his voice.

"Yeah." Though he would have faked it before, since he started hanging out with Charlie, he was more confident. He was going for his first parachute jump in the morning before his run with Charlie, and he had no reason to think he couldn't do it, especially after yesterday's bungee success. "I've got this. I'll see you guys then."

Lance grinned. "Great. Later."

As Lance and Dak took off, leaving Hunter alone, his doubts filled the silence. After the run, he could definitely keep up with the other jumpers. But was his head in the game, too?

Tomorrow, he was going to find out.

Chapter Seven

He couldn't do this.

Hunter pulled over at the next emergency pull-off and shifted into park. He refused to turn off the engine, though. Whatever panic was coursing through him was going to stop. He only needed to wait it out.

Tell that to his racing heart and shaking hands.

He was only a few miles from the Bend Municipal Airport, but the distance seemed impassable. It was the distance between thinking you could do something and recognizing that you couldn't.

His appointment to jump—his first parachute since the day he'd been injured—was in two hours.

He still wasn't sure he was going to make it.

Why the hell was he putting himself through this? He hadn't slept last night, too worried about everything that could go wrong. Every time he got close to falling asleep, his body jolted as if muscle memory was reminding him of how it felt to fall through the sky. He would jerk awake, sweating and cursing, tears running down his cheeks.

It wasn't only the fear and panic—it was the weakness that was breaking him.

All morning, he had considered rescheduling dozens of times. He still had about a week before he had to show up at the air center for the first day of training. Jumping on no sleep wasn't ideal. It would probably be best to wait until he was better rested.

Except that frightened him worst of all. Because he was beginning to wonder if he would ever want to jump. If maybe parachuting was something in his past.

His fear that he would never jump again outweighed his fear of the parachute today. He refused to be a failure. He'd come too far to quit now.

God, he was glad no one was witnessing this. He had considered inviting Lance or Dak to come with him. Not that they needed any practice jumping. The veteran smokejumpers had probably already been in the sky a dozen times this spring. They would have come with him, though, if he had asked. If they were with him right now, he doubted he would be on the side of the road, shaking like a fucking sissy. He would shut his mouth and push through.

Sure, he might have had a panic attack in the sky, but he would've made it there.

No, he didn't ask them because then he would've had to explain how fucked up he had become.

They wouldn't judge him. He knew them both well enough to know they would understand. At least they would understand that he was struggling, facing what had happened last year. They would be supportive. They would give him a bunch of lip service about how this didn't make him any less of a firefighter. How he was still strong.

But they would pity him. He would watch it wash over their faces, how bad they felt for him. While they spoke words of encouragement, they would think that he might never be the same again.

He didn't need to see those concerns on their faces. He faced that shit every day in the mirror.

A car passed, slowing down, and the driver turned toward him, obviously checking to make sure Hunter was okay.

Was he okay? He wasn't sure if he knew what okay felt like anymore.

Images of Charlie's face sprang to mind. Her kind eyes, the way the skin wrinkled around them when she smiled up at him. The incredulous widening of them when he did something she thought was insane.

The soft curve of her lovely cheek.

In spite of his still-racing pulse, he smiled.

Charlie understood him. She might not get exactly why he did the things he did, but there was something unspoken there. Something in sync between them. Something he needed.

He was coming to depend on her too much. It was dangerous, relying on her for this sort of comfort. More, it wasn't fair to her. She had no idea that he looked to her for peace or that she'd helped him stop panic from controlling him on two important occasions over the past week.

But despite all of that—despite how he was worried that he was using her, that it scared the shit out of him that she had this much control over his emotions—he needed her.

He would figure out what all of that meant after he figured out how to jump out of a plane again without losing his shit.

One thing was certain: he wasn't going to make it into the sky today if she wasn't there.

He checked his watch. It was ten o'clock in the morning. She'd be at the office.

Checking his rearview mirror, he signaled and U-turned in the street, heading back toward Bend.

* * * *

Charlie was finishing with Mr. Underwood's hip workout when the bell on the door chimed. Glancing up, she caught sight of Hunter, filling out the doorframe.

Was she ever going to get used to how incredibly attractive he was? It wasn't only that he was in peak physical shape. She worked out, she ran and lifted, spent time at the gym with lots of other people who were physically fit. Oregon was coated in amazing trails and outdoor spaces as well. People used them.

No, it wasn't only that he was muscled and tall and broad. There was something too appealing about his gaze. When he looked at her, she got the impression that he saw her. That he didn't only put together the pieces of her body, her arms and legs, and whether he liked the shape of her. He saw through that, to whatever it was in the heart of her.

For a girl who had been searching for connection her entire life, what she saw in his eyes attracted her like a moth to a flame.

What was he doing there? Their plans to go for a run weren't for a couple of hours. She still had another patient before the end of her day.

"Mr. Underwood? Could you give me a second?" When the older man waved a hand, she helped him to a seat. She figured he'd been fine to take a brief break. He was already sweating and cursing at her. He'd been recommended to the practice after surgery, and he hated it. His wife had bribed him to come today with the promise of a hamburger.

Reaching for her towel, she strolled over to the door. "Hey," she greeted Hunter, trying to sound casual. "What are you doing here? We aren't supposed to meet until later today."

"Right." He glanced at Mr. Underwood. "Yeah, I'm a little early."

"A couple hours early." She narrowed her eyes. "I don't think you forgot how to read a watch."

"I definitely didn't." He wasn't grinning. If anything, he looked freaked out.

"You just in the neighborhood?" she coaxed, when he didn't continue. Whatever was going on with him, she got the impression she should tread lightly.

"No. I mean, yes. But not exactly." He ran a hand over his hair, the fingers digging in.

"Spit it out, Hunter." She nudged her head toward Mr. Underwood. "I have to get back to my patient. What's going on?"

He crossed his arms over his chest, leaning in so only she could hear. "I need you to come and jump out of a plane with me."

She blinked at him. "I'm sorry, what?"

"Hear me out." He took her by the bicep, leading her away from where Mrs. Underwood was sitting in the waiting area, trying to pretend she wasn't listening. When they were out of hearing, Hunter's gaze strayed to where he was holding Charlie, and he dropped his fingers. "Listen, you liked the bungee jumping, right?"

He paused, so she nodded. She had to admit, it had been fun. Something she'd never expected to do or like.

"Right, so if you liked that, you're probably going to like parachuting."

"Whoa." She lifted her hands. "First of all, they are two very different things."

"Well, not exactly—"

"And second," she interrupted. "I've got clients today. You told me that you were going this morning."

"I am. Right now."

"You want me to leave my clients and go jump out of an airplane with you? Right now?"

"Well, not exactly. I can wait for you to finish."

She could only stare at him. "Are you sure you didn't hit your head while we were bungee jumping?"

He laughed, and the sound of it struck her low in her belly. God, this man. Why did she have to find everything about him so goddamned attractive? In front of her, he was a solid wall of muscle. Not only muscle, but wonderful-smelling muscle. His scent was warm and spicy, with cologne or something. She couldn't pinpoint what it was, but she suspected it was something uniquely his.

As if unaware of what his proximity was doing to her, he continued. "It's much easier and more fun to go with someone else."

Even though she ran through the million ways this was illogical, excitement trickled through her. She could see it, tucking her hand in his, the wild and wonderful sensation of heading off to do something unadvised. Something just a little crazy.

But she couldn't ignore all the ways it didn't make sense for him to be there.

"Come on, Hunter. You can't tell me that there aren't a dozen other people you know who would be more than happy to go jump out of a plane with you." Unwittingly, images of the kinds of girls she'd seen staring at him—women of every age, shape, and size—burst into her head. She shook them away. "I mean, your friends. Lance, Dak. They would go. Why aren't you somewhere asking them to do death-defying things with you?"

"Because you're who I want to do death-defying things with." He attempted to make it sound casual, teasing even, but she caught the seriousness underneath. Looking up into his eyes, she recognized that this wasn't a spur-of-the-moment decision to come and convince her to go. There was something else there.

"Me?"

"Yeah." His gaze fell away from her, drifting over her shoulder. "And I can't ask them." His words were low, quiet and tortured. "They don't get it."

"Your friends?" she whispered. "They don't get what?"

"They feel bad for me." He smirked. "The parachute that failed me had been sabotaged, but it had been meant for Lance. I picked it up. It could have been anyone else who could have picked it up. They're all supposed to be packed exactly the same. We'd set our stuff out, prepared it for our jump. It had been a mistake for me to get the bag." He narrowed his eyes. "Imagine how they must feel? Lance, who was supposed to have been the one with the messed-up bag. Dak, who was on that plane, too."

"They pity you. And they feel guilty." Of course they did. How wouldn't they? She'd read that Lance had tried to save Hunter, that he was the only reason Hunter was still alive. Yet, Hunter had still been horribly injured. There had been talk back then that he might not walk again. It must be hard for Lance to watch his friend struggle to recover. He would always wonder if there was something else he could have done, something that might have changed the outcome for the better.

"I try not to let on how hard things have been." Hunter turned, paced away. She got the impression he wanted to put some distance between them, too. That this was difficult for him to talk about. "I don't want them to feel like this is, well, their fault."

"It's not their fault. But it isn't your fault either." It was important that he remember that, that he hadn't chosen this path either.

As she watched him, her admiration grew. This man had been through hell. She'd seen the aftermath of injuries like his. She'd witnessed the pain and stiffness, the frustration when one's limbs didn't behave how their owner wanted them to. It was humbling and angering; she'd seen it. For him to go from where he'd been a year ago to where he was now, it must have taken a huge amount of determination.

He had a quiet strength about him, a solid core. Watching him struggle with vulnerability, to be struck down by fear, was hard for her.

But could she do what he was asking her to do? She'd bungee-jumped, but this? She'd need to get into a plane, wear a parachute on her back. She'd need to jump out of the plane and put her faith in that pack to save her life.

Looking into Hunter's eyes, she realized she didn't have nearly the fear to overcome that he did. And if he could entertain the thought of going up there and jumping, then she could, too.

"After I'm done here." She motioned toward Mr. Underwood and his wife. "This client is finished in fifteen or so, and I have one more after that."

His exhale was full of relief. "Of course." He grinned. "That would be great."

While she finished up, she was acutely aware of his eyes on her. When her last patient left, she checked in with Leslie who was working a client through some exercises. "See you later, Leslie. I've got to go parachuting."

Leslie glanced behind her to where Hunter was standing. "I'm sorry, what?"

"Parachuting."

Her boss blinked. "Huh."

That was all she said. Charlie scowled at her. "What does that mean?" Last time she checked, "huh" wasn't a real statement.

"He's a good fit for you."

She stilled. "Oh, no. It's not like that. He needs someone to go with him. To jump out of a plane."

"Right. Of course. That makes complete sense." Leslie rolled her eyes.

The client Leslie was helping to stretch clicked her tongue. "Honey, no one jumps out of a plane for someone unless they like them."

"I agree, Janice." Leslie barely contained her chuckle.

"He's my friend's brother." It was the last logical argument, and it still wasn't that much of one. As her gaze strayed to Hunter, standing near the door, she could see how this might give her boss the wrong idea. Hunter had other people to ask. He'd come to her. Was there more there than she was willing to admit?

Maybe. She didn't know. But there was no way she was going to let that man down. He'd already come too far. If having her come along made him get over whatever last hang-ups he had, then so be it. "I'll see you tomorrow." Charlie waved as she backed away. "Have a good day, Ms. Lloyd."

"You too, dear," the woman offered from her deep quad stretch on the table.

"See you tomorrow, Char." Leslie grinned, winking. "And have fun."

As Charlie waved goodbye, she met Hunter's eyes and nodded.

The smile that split his lips was brighter than the sun.

Chapter Eight

As the plane reached jumping altitude, Charlie's skin looked pale and her eyes were wide. Though most of the time she didn't stop talking, now she was completely silent.

She looked like she might throw up.

Not for the first time, Hunter regretted dragging her into this. He should have never convinced her to do this. He should have let her off the hook, told her that she was right, that it was okay, that he could do this on his own. That he didn't need her there for moral support.

He'd have been lying, but that's what he should have done.

"You don't have to jump," he offered for the third time. "The pilot is going right back to the airport. You don't have to do this."

She looked him over. Her eyes scanned his face, quick, assessing. He had no idea what she saw there, but she shook her head. "No. I'm going."

"Seriously. I'm good. I'm going."

"I know." She nodded. "You're good because you're worrying about me. You're not freaking out because you're too busy worrying about my freaking out."

He could only stare at her. Was that what was happening here? Had he dragged her up here to take his place in the panic? "That's not it at all."

"Are you sure?" She grinned, but she still looked a little sick. "Because that's how it feels to me."

"I'm sure. I brought you here because you make me happy." He was yelling over the motor, but he didn't care. "I brought you because when you look at me, I feel like I'm as strong as you think I am."

Maybe he should have been embarrassed by the words. They were super sappy for a guy who wasn't into talking about his feelings. But when she smiled—a real smile, not the sick one from before—he decided he didn't care. The words had been worth it.

"Then you can jump first, big guy. Show me how it's done." She pointed to the window and wiggled her eyebrows. Something about the ridiculousness of it made him laugh.

"Fine. I'll go first. As long as you promise to meet me down there." He shouldn't be daring her, but with her dark curls wild around her face and the color returning to her cheeks, she was delicious.

She stuck her hand out to him. "Deal."

Encasing her fingers in his, he held them too long. God, he wanted to touch her, to taste her. And that he was thinking about that here, at twelve thousand feet, instead of worrying about losing his lunch, well, it was pretty amazing.

The parachuting instructor motioned to him. As they moved through the pre-jump procedure, he couldn't keep his eyes from straying toward her. She believed he could do this. He could see it on her face. She was afraid, probably even understood how terrified he was, but she had faith in him.

He wasn't going to let her down.

As he stepped into the doorway, he stared out into the open air in front of him. He sat down, his feet dangling. His stomach lurched, but it wasn't much worse than he remembered from past jumps. His gaze found the horizon, and he marveled again at the beauty here. This was what had drawn him to parachuting, the thing he'd kept coming back to all those years.

He could do this. He might have told her that to calm her, to keep her from worrying. But it was true. He was here, in front of the sky, and he could definitely do this.

Turning, he offered her a salute. She tilted her head in acknowledgment. With that, he threw himself out the door.

The first five seconds as he waited for his parachute to engage were torturous. He wondered if he'd told his mother, his sister, his friends that he loved them. If they would know if he didn't make it back to them alive. Maybe some people would find that morbid, but he'd been too close to death before to take such things for granted.

The familiar tug of the parachute opening lifted his stomach, and he was floating. Only then did he allow himself to look around, to breathe in the silence and joy that came when a man floated alone in the atmosphere.

Except he wasn't alone. Charlie was coming down with him.

Had she made it? He craned his head, adjusting to see if he could find her parachute in the sky above him. When he couldn't find her, the familiar sensation hit him—the increased heart rate, the sweaty palms.

Oh, God, please let her be safe.

There, though. To the east, he caught sight of another chute. He laughed then, letting out the pent-up energy that had been flowing inside him. They'd done it, jumped out of the plane. After all these months, wondering if he could, if he should, he'd finally done it.

And it was glorious.

As he maneuvered the landing, cushioning himself from hurting his knees, he was laughing and swiping at the moisture on his cheeks.

He'd done it. There was nothing holding him back now. He would go to training next week, become a smokejumper like he'd always planned.

As Charlie landed a few hundred yards away, he watched her lift her fists in triumph.

Damned if he didn't know exactly what that felt like.

* * * *

"So do you think you're going to want to go parachuting with me again?" Next to her, Hunter buried his hands in his pockets. With his backpack on, his sun-bleached hair, and his tan, he looked more like a frat boy than a man about to begin training to be an elite firefighter.

He was full of those kinds of contradictions, it seemed.

"I don't think so." She chuckled. "I'll leave the high-altitude theatrics to you guys."

He laughed as they reached her Honda and she pulled her keys from her bag, unlocking it.

As awkwardness settled over them, she gazed toward the sunset. Staring into the sun was easier than looking directly at him.

"Thanks for convincing me to try this." She waved toward the airport. "I would have never attempted that without you."

His smile slipped away, replaced by the seriousness that always seemed to be right below his surface. "No, thank you for coming with me. You don't know how much it means to me." His gaze held hers, his blue eyes so intense that she resisted the urge to look away, to hide from him. Except she couldn't. She never seemed to be able to keep things light with this man. She needed to try harder.

"You're welcome." She cleared her throat, motioning to her car but still unable to look away. "You don't need me for training, do you?"

He shook his head. "No, not anymore."

Nodding, she swallowed. "Your smokejumper training starts soon, right?"

"I am supposed to be there next Sunday." He stepped closer, forcing her to look up at him.

"Then I guess I'll see you around." She tried to give him a bright smile, to keep things friendly and professional, but it was hard with him standing next to her. "This was a lot of fun."

"Charlie?" he whispered, her name sounding entirely too good on his lips.

"Yeah?" Was that her voice, all breathy like that? Had she meant it to sound so sexy?

"You said our training is over, right?"

"I did." God, he was so close. Everything in her vibrated.

He ran his hand along her shoulders. He didn't exert any pressure, but she leaned closer as if he had. "So if I wanted to kiss you, it wouldn't be unprofessional now, would it?"

Her breathing hitched, and it was impossible to speak. Instead, she shook her head.

"Would it be okay, then? To kiss you?"

"Yes." The word escaped her on the breath she'd been holding. He held her gaze, lowered his head, and covered her mouth with his. Her eyes fluttered closed.

It wasn't until his lips moved against hers that she recognized how much she'd wanted this. The past week or so, awareness had zinged between them, some connection she'd been unable to ignore. Now, as he pulled her closer and her body folded into his, fitting perfectly, she couldn't deny how that connection wasn't only a syncing of their emotions but something better. Hotter.

Her fingers trailed up his back, pressing into the muscles there as her stomach dropped and her entire existence seemed to center on the places their bodies met. Their mouths, their thighs, her chest against his. She gripped his T-shirt, pulling it as she tilted her head. His lips were warm, his tongue gentle but consuming. She sighed, allowing herself to bend into him, to feel him with as much of herself as she could.

One of his hands trailed across her neck and into the hair at the back of her head. He used that big palm to angle her, to gain better access to her mouth, and she let him. Hell, she didn't only allow it; she craved it.

When he lifted his mouth from hers, he didn't step back, only held her against him, his hand brushing her hair out of her face as he stared into her eyes. What she saw there was so intense and full of meaning that she couldn't keep looking at him. Dropping her gaze and her hands, she stepped away from him. But he gripped her wrists, as if he didn't want her to go far.

"Charlie—"

"Hunter, please. Let me." She shook her head. "That was amazing." That didn't seem to cover it, but it was the best word she could find with her head still scrambled. "But I probably shouldn't have kissed you. I don't know that this, whatever is here between us, is a good idea."

"What do you mean?" His voice was clipped and his brow crinkled.

Didn't he get it? "Your sister is my best friend. You don't just go around kissing your best friend's brother."

"Well, I think we already proved that we do." The corner of his mouth tilted up.

She scowled at him. "I don't think you're getting the full scope of this."

"And I think you're blowing it way out of proportion."

She couldn't help it; she flinched. Though she tried to hide it, to remain still, she could tell he noticed because he hurried to add, "I mean—"

"No, I know what you mean." He meant that it was a kiss, not a marriage proposal. And she got that, she did. She wasn't some naïve teenager. She'd had relationships, even important ones. Except what he said was right. She always took things too seriously, too fast. Sure this was just one kiss with the brother of her friend. But she could see how this could become something much bigger and more important.

At least to her. Which was the real problem, wasn't it? She wasn't the sort to shield her heart. She should have learned this lesson after Joshua.

Apparently she hadn't.

She tried for a casual smile, something that said she wasn't that affected. She hoped she succeeded. "You're about to start an important phase of your career. Smokejumper training is about a month, right?"

His glare didn't change as he nodded.

"You don't have time for anything right now, do you? And you need to be focused on your career. Not on other things." Her argument made sense. He had to see that this wouldn't be a good idea. Not for either of them.

Especially not for her.

His hands fell away, dropping to his sides, as the scowl remained on his face. "I see what you mean."

The words pierced through her, laced with relief. How could she be upset and relieved at the same time? And that was the exact sort of mixed-up crazy that explained why she couldn't take a chance with him.

She squeezed his hand. "Truly, you should think about yourself right now." She dropped her fingers, even as she wanted to keep holding his. "I'll see you around, though, right?"

"Yeah, Charlie." He nodded, his jaw tight. "Sure. See you around."

With nothing left to say, she slipped into her car. As she pulled out of the parking lot, she couldn't resist looking in the rearview mirror. Hunter was where she had left him, watching her drive away.

Chapter Nine

"Hey, Hunt. Hang on."

Hunter paused beside his TrailBlazer, half his stuff on the ground. Meg ran up beside him, still in her training gear. She and the other trainers had run the smokejumper recruits through one of the more rigorous sessions this afternoon. Three weeks ago, at the beginning of training, he would have found it challenging. Today, though, he'd been pleased at how little he ached afterward.

He'd come a long way since the start of training.

It hadn't hurt that he'd thrown himself into it completely. It wasn't only that he'd been planning all year for this, though that had been part of it. No, it had helped him take his mind off how badly he'd crashed and burned with Charlie.

Still, three weeks later, he had to fight the urge every day to call or text her.

"Hey, Meg. You leaving?"

"Not yet." She jerked a thumb toward the air center. "I've got paperwork to do." She tucked her arms around her, probably chilled in the cool air. That week had been unseasonably cool. Not that he was complaining. It was way easier to work out without starting off sweating his butt off.

She grinned, rocking back on her heels. "You're doing great, you know."

He did know, but he was glad she'd noticed. That was the important part. "Thanks."

"No, seriously. You're top of the class."

He knew that, too, but while he should have found a lot more satisfaction in that, he could only work up exhaustion. It had been tough, but it was almost guaranteed that he was going to graduate next week, unless something unforeseen happened. He'd expected that would fill him with victory, triumph. Something. Instead, training had been anticlimactic.

Maybe it was that he'd worked so hard this past year to get there that he'd built it up too much in his head. It wasn't as if he wasn't proud of himself. He was. It was only that he'd expected to feel like a conquering hero. Instead, it only seemed like the next logical step. Something he'd expected to accomplish, not something greater than that.

He hadn't given himself much time to ponder it, though. He'd been too busy. In a week, training would be over and he'd be a smokejumper, like his father before him. Like his brother and uncle had been.

Like he was supposed to be.

"Thanks." He grinned at his sister. "So what's up? You just come out to give me a pat on the back?" He continued loading his car.

"Actually, I was wondering if Lance had gotten a chance to invite you over tomorrow."

"Tomorrow?" He shook his head. "I haven't seen much of Lance this week." He'd been so busy with training, and Lance had been with the other veteran jumpers. Their paths hadn't crossed much. At least not enough to give them time to catch up.

"Oh. Well, then, that's good. Because I kind of wanted to talk to you first."

He narrowed his eyes. "Meg, you're acting weird. Are you sick?"

"No." Her face split into a huge grin, and she bounced on the balls of her feet. "But I am getting married." She followed that announcement with a muted squeal, hitting a note he couldn't imagine reaching.

Then they were laughing, hugging in the middle of the parking lot at RAC. He rubbed his chin against his sister's red hair. In the months after his accident, he had had moments of thankfulness to be alive. They'd come at strange times, over a particularly good cup of coffee or when his younger twin brothers asked him to play video games with them. That had faded some, maybe because the accident wasn't as fresh, but when the moments did creep up on him, they stole his breath.

He was here, watching his sister's happiness. What a gift.

Meg pulled back, swiping at the corner of her eye, still grinning like a fool. "That's why we're having some people over tomorrow night. I hope you can come."

"Wouldn't miss it."

"Great. Keep it quiet, though? It's kind of a housewarming, too. But not formal. So no gifts or anything. It just would mean a lot to me if you could be there." She and Lance had closed on a house in Bend two weeks ago. He'd helped them move their furniture. Since Lance hadn't come to

Redmond with much and Meg was moving from a one-bedroom apartment, it hadn't taken long.

"Absolutely. I'd love to." He winked at her. "I'll be sure to catch up on my sleep in the morning. My trainer here?" He nudged his head toward the building. "She's a real ballbuster."

Meg laughed. "Yeah, I hear she's the worst."

He grinned, tweaking her ponytail like he had when they were kids. He loved seeing her this happy. "She's all right."

He might have been mistaken, but her eyes seemed to get watery. Before he fell into full panic, though, she blinked a couple of times, hard. "I'm serious about training, Hunt. I'm proud of you."

It was him, then, who got choked up. Over the past year, he'd guessed that Meg had worried about him. She'd tried not to mother, leaving the real nagging to their mom. But he'd caught her concerned looks, the tightness around her eyes sometimes. He'd done what he could to keep the bulk of his trials and troubles to himself. But she was his sister. She'd been bound to notice.

"Thanks, Meggy." He leaned forward, folding her into a quick hug. "I love you," he whispered in her ear.

"I love you more, you jackass."

He chuckled, pulling away and finishing throwing his stuff in the back of the SUV, giving them a second to pull it together. Then, as casually as he could, he asked, "So, is Charlie coming?"

Though there had been no way he could avoid asking, when he watched renewed concern light his sister's eyes, he immediately regretted it. He hurried to add, "I haven't talked to her in a while. I was just wondering how she was."

"She's good. She stopped over a few days ago, dropped off a pie." He might have been mistaken, but she almost sounded apologetic. "And yeah, she's going to be there."

A zing of anticipation passed through him, but he was sure he kept it off his features. Meg didn't need to know how much he'd been looking forward to seeing Charlie again.

After they parachuted, he'd been sure that they'd turned a corner. There was definitely something between them. He could sense it, simmering there. When he'd asked to kiss her, he'd seen how much she wanted that, too.

God, that kiss. There had been chemistry between them, but the force of it had nearly sent him to his knees. He'd never wanted to let her go.

But then it had all fallen apart. She'd immediately pulled away, not only physically but emotionally. She'd given him a whole string of reasons why they needed to forget that kiss had happened. His sister, training,

whatever. It had been bullshit. If anything, missing her had been the biggest
distraction he'd faced during training.

And he did miss her. At night, he lay awake, wondering what she was
doing, remembering her smile, her wild curls. The way her curves had
fit against him.

He didn't know much about her, but he wanted to.

"Good," he finally said. "That's good."

He closed the hatch on the SUV, offering his sister a wave goodbye.
"I'll see you tomorrow, then. Text me if you need anything."

"I will." She stepped back. "But Hunter?"

He paused, his brows lifted. "Yeah?"

"It's Charlie." She stopped, worrying her lower lip. "I wanted to tell you—"

Sudden panic overtook him. "Wait. Does she have a boyfriend?" The
idea was so incongruous to what he had sensed about her. She didn't strike
him as the kind of woman to kiss another man while dating someone else,
but he never claimed to understand people. Maybe he'd read her all wrong.

"Oh, God no." Meg laughed, and the relief that flooded him made him
weak. Thank God. "No, no boyfriend. But, that's kind of what I wanted
to say. Charlie is private."

"I know." Even though she wasn't shy, she never seemed to reveal
much about herself.

"No, I mean really private. We've been friends for years and I still don't
know much about her."

"What do you mean?"

Meg inhaled. "She came from Chicago. I think. But I get the impression
that isn't where she grew up. When I've asked where she grew up, she has
said 'everywhere.'"

"Everywhere?" He cocked his head. "Was she an Army brat or something?"

"I don't think so." She shrugged. "Honestly, I have no idea. That's what
I mean. She doesn't say much, and when I ask, she deflects. She's good
at changing the subject, turning things back to me. She wants to know
everything about everyone else. She's the most selfless conversationalist in
the world, probably one of the most selfless people I've ever met. But I just
wanted you to know. You have your own things. I think Charlie does, too."

He didn't want to get into what his own things were, not here, not with
Meg. So he nodded. "I'll keep that in mind."

She smiled. "Good. That's all I wanted."

He waved again, climbing into the driver's seat as she headed
back to the RAC.

He'd guessed that Charlie wasn't comfortable talking about herself. He'd gotten tastes of it during their bungee jump and parachuting, but he'd never suspected that it went any deeper than a desire to keep to herself.

Now, though, he wondered if there were other reasons she'd panicked after their kiss.

Well, tomorrow he'd get another chance to try to figure out Charlie Jones. It was disconcerting how much he was looking forward to it.

* * * *

Charlie's cell was on the fourth ring when she swiped to answer it. "Hello?"

She hadn't heard it in the bathroom because she'd been drying her hair. She didn't usually blow it out, because she was naturally curly and it was easier to let it do its thing instead of forcing it to be something it wasn't meant to. But tonight, she wanted it to look exactly right.

Meg's party. Hunter was going to be there.

"Charlie? Is that you?"

"Leslie?" She tucked the phone under her ear. "Hey. How are you?"

Leslie had called out again yesterday from work. Charlie was starting to worry. Maybe it was time she got bloodwork or something.

"I'm pregnant."

Charlie halted on her way through the kitchen of her apartment. "You are?" The words were squeaked out in her excitement, and she jumped up and down. "Oh my God, that's wonderful. No wonder you've been so sick. I was going to suggest you get in for a physical."

"Oh, I've been for some physicals. Trust me, I think they've looked at every crevice." Leslie laughed, her joy apparent even over the phone line.

Charlie joined in. "I bet. Is everything going well?"

"I'm perfectly healthy. And Kyle and I are over the moon. We've been trying to get pregnant for almost a year."

"I had no idea. I'm so happy for you." She was. Charlie loved babies. She couldn't wait to be a mother. Her relationship with her parents was unorthodox, but they adored her. She wanted that feeling of belonging to someone.

Maybe someday she'd get it.

"I didn't want to tell you until we were past the first trimester, but now that we are, I wanted to explain why I've been a flake the past couple of months."

"No need. I get it."

"And I wanted to tell you that I'll be pulling back on some of my hours at work." Leslie exhaled. "I figured that this was a good time for us to have a conversation that is probably about a year overdue."

"What's that?" Charlie reached for the stack of mail on her table, riffling through the envelopes and flyers. Bills, mostly. A couple of coupons to department stores.

"I know you've been saving to start your own therapy practice." Leslie paused. "Instead of doing that, I was wondering if you'd be interested in buying into ours."

Charlie lowered the mail to the table. "Are you serious?" According to her business plan, she would be able to begin her own meager practice next year. She'd been living in her small one-bedroom and taking on personal training clients at every opportunity, but she'd begun to wonder if her goal wasn't a lifetime away. If her own shop would ever be a reality.

But this? She might have enough now, depending on what Leslie's number might be. "What were you thinking?"

"I already discussed it with Becky, and we have a proposal to send over. In the meantime, I think that the price range we're looking at is reasonable." She named a figure that wasn't far from what was already in Charlie's portfolio.

Excitement squeezed her stomach, even as she tried to keep herself from squealing. She could do this. She could buy in, have her name on a plaque, and be part of something. Create a home here, in Oregon.

Maybe someday she could start a family, too, like Leslie and Kyle.

As she straightened her mail, trying to contain her nervous energy, an envelope caught her eye. Her first name—Charlie—was scribbled across the front of it. Maybe it was from her landlord. Slipping her finger under the flap, she said, "I'm looking forward to seeing the proposal, Leslie, but..."

Her voice trailed off as she pulled the single piece of paper from the envelope. It was an advertisement for a gun.

Why the hell would someone send her an ad for a pistol? She didn't own a gun, having read too many statistics about how people were more likely to have their own gun used against them than to protect themselves with it.

Flipping the paper—what looked to be a page from a magazine—she found a sticky note with the words "You should consider one."

The page slid from her fingers, fluttering to the table.

"Charlie? Are you there?"

She hadn't responded to Leslie, letting the pause get too awkward. She adjusted her grip on the phone. "I'm here. Sorry about that. Like I said,

I'm looking forward to seeing the proposal, Les, but I'll need to talk with my attorney. I'll definitely let you know."

Though they were the same words that she'd planned when Leslie had given her the figure, now they were only a formality. She would be checking with her attorney, but now it would be to see if this could be traced back to Joshua. To make sure she was still safe.

Was this from Joshua? It didn't seem like something he would do, but it had been a few years. She had no idea how he had changed.

She wished Leslie good health again, hanging up. The paper in front of her taunted her. Maybe it was nothing. There were plenty of people who knew about the drug addict who had tried to steal her money a few weeks ago. This could be one of her well-meaning patients, thinking she should protect herself. But she couldn't ignore the chance that it was something more.

Briefly, she wondered if she should call the police. But there was nothing overtly threatening. It was an ad, for heaven's sake. And a suggestion. But what that piece of paper had done was something dangerous. It had sucked away her earlier excitement at Leslie's proposal. How was she supposed to consider setting down roots if stuff like this was going to happen to her?

Maybe it was nothing. She shouldn't panic. What she should do was call her attorney, see what she had to say.

Picking up her phone, she dialed her attorney. When the woman picked up, Charlie said, "Hey, Peggy. It's Charlotte Michaelson. It's been a while. Listen, something happened and I was hoping you'd look into it for me."

Then she walked to her front door and checked all her locks. Just to be sure.

Chapter Ten

As Hunter stepped inside Meg and Lance's new place, a lovely ranch in a subdivision, he could hear the music, but it wasn't loud enough to overpower conversation. The three-bedroom new construction Lance and Meg had bought near the Bend hospital was full of people. It had only been a couple of weeks, but the place looked settled. Meg was a bit of a cleaning and organizing machine, though. He bet she hadn't been able to sleep with things in chaos around her.

Across the room, he caught Dak Parrish's gaze and he weaved between the bodies to join him. Snagging a beer as he passed a side table, he shook Dak's hand and scanned the room for Charlie as he made hey-man-how-you-doings small talk.

"I'm going to ask Heidi to move in with me."

The statement made Hunter jerk out of his eye-wandering and pay attention to what his buddy was saying. "You are? Congratulations."

Next to him, Dak sipped his beer, gazing across the room at his girlfriend. Heidi Sinclair was a Forest Services investigator, and the two of them had been together since the fall. "Now that the season is starting again and things will pick up with her job, I don't want to spend any more time than necessary away from her."

There were a lot of guys who couldn't admit that they didn't want to be parted from the women they loved. That Dak stated it like it was a well-acknowledged fact made Hunter respect him even more. "Don't blame you. Heidi's great." He took a drink from his own bottle. "If I were you, I wouldn't want to waste time driving back and forth between your places either."

Dak shrugged. "I only need to figure out about the garage." Since the end of the fire season last year, Dak had been working with his brother at a garage on the Warm Springs Tribal Reservation. They'd talked about opening their own place, but Mikey didn't want to leave the reservation, and Dak would need to be closer to Redmond.

"I'm sure you guys will figure it out."

"We've been through worse."

That they had. Last fall, their mother had been arrested for arson after struggling with mental illness for years. Dak's family was still working through all of the ripple effects, but one thing that had come out of it was a strengthened relationship between the brothers.

Hunter and Dak had a mostly unspoken bond over shared dysfunctional sibling relationships. He hadn't contacted his own brother, Will, since Will had purposely twisted the parachute that had nearly killed him. Will had spent a few months in jail, and then he'd been on probation and working with an outpatient mental health facility. Though Meg and their mother had spoken with Will, Hunter wasn't ready yet.

He might not ever be ready.

He scanned the room. He didn't see Charlie. She was late. Was she okay? Then again, he would have no idea if she'd canceled, if she'd texted Meg to tell her that she was running behind. He wasn't privy to the details of her life.

He wished he were, though.

"Excuse me, everyone." Lance tapped the side of his beer glass. The chatter in the room died, as the guests turned to face him. Hunter crossed his arms over his chest, grinning. Here it came. The big announcement. He skimmed the partygoers, wondering if any of them were suspecting the engagement announcement.

That's when Hunter saw her.

She must have only arrived, because she was shrugging out of the light jacket she'd worn as she spoke with one of Meg's other friends from Bend, Olivia. Charlie's hair was pulled back with pins or something, the curls more tamed than usual. In jeans and some sort of ruffly, bohemian-style top, she struck that chord between cute and sexy.

He had taken two steps toward her before he caught himself.

"Thank you all for coming," Lance said, drawing his attention. Hunter's sister stood next to her boyfriend, and Lance wrapped his arm around her shoulder, pulling her to his side. "Meg and I just moved in a couple of weeks ago, and we're excited to start our life here in Bend together. We also wanted to wait until we had you all here to make this announcement."

He inhaled, and the smile on his face matched the beaming on his sister's. "The night we moved in, I asked Meg to be my wife. I'm humbled to say that she agreed. We'll be getting married in the fall."

The room erupted into cheers and happy shouts of congratulations. Hunter lifted his beer bottle, calling over the crowd, "To Meg and Lance. Cheers."

Around him, others did the same, repeating the toast. Across the room, he caught Lance's attention, touching his eyebrow to his friend in salute. If someone had told him two years ago that he'd be so happy at the prospect of adding Lance Roberts to his family, he would have laughed. When he had returned to Oregon last spring, their hometown had still assumed Lance's father had caused the death of Hunter and Meg's father as well as his own.

After everything they'd been through, Hunter couldn't have been happier for him and Meg.

As friends and family pressed forward to offer more personal congratulations, Hunter's gaze found Charlie's. Like every time that they'd made eye contact, something connected between them, something warm and welcome. He tilted his bottle toward her and she grinned, weaving through the outskirts of well-wishers.

"Hey, you," she offered. "Congratulations on the soon-to-be brother-in-law."

"Thanks." Across the room, the couple in question beamed, hugging well-wishers. "They're a good fit. Always have been."

Her eyes narrowed. "Always?"

"You think a guy doesn't notice when his best friend is in love with his sister?" He winked at her. "I always suspected how Lance felt in high school. I wasn't sure about Meg, though. And she's my sister. That wasn't something I could have asked her back then." He shrugged. "It all figured itself out in the end."

"I'm excited for them," Charlie said, her eyes on her friend. "She deserves this happiness."

Lance couldn't agree more, but he couldn't stop his flare of jealousy. Since training last year, Meg and Lance had built a relationship, one they would continue to grow into their marriage. They'd purchased a home, created a life.

Him? He'd spent the past year recovering from grave injuries and waiting to finish rookie training, to pick up where his life had left off. And now that he was so close to the end, he couldn't help wondering if all that effort had been worth it. In two weeks, he'd be a full-fledged smokejumper. That had been his dream since he was a child, and the desire to fulfill that goal had only become more intense over the past year, when he believed he wouldn't be able to accomplish it.

Now, though, on the cusp of attaining his objective, he was starting to question if this was all there was.

"I was wondering if you were still coming," he said softly. "Meg had told me you'd be here, but I thought maybe something came up."

"Surely you weren't waiting for me, Hunter Buchanan?" Charlie teased, snagging a glass of champagne from a tray someone had brought from the kitchen.

"I was." He didn't want to pretend. "I wanted to see you."

Her smile faded, and her features became troubled. "It's good to see you, too, but I can't—"

"We can talk, right?" He needed a chance to talk with her, to catch up. He wanted to know what was going on with her more than anything.

She paused, biting her lip. He waited. Ultimately, it was up to her. Either she wanted to know him, or she didn't.

"Yes," she finally said. "Yes, we can."

He exhaled, overwhelmed with relief. "Great." He glanced at Lance and Meg, still swarmed by people. "Why don't we hang out on the patio for a little bit? It might be a while before we can say congrats to the happy couple."

She nodded. He offered her his hand and, after a moment's hesitation, she slipped her fingers into his. Turning, he led them out the French doors.

* * * *

As the cool night air, a welcome respite from the heat inside, hit Charlie, it brought with it a rush of reality.

Why had she allowed herself to come out here on the patio with Hunter?

She could have made up an excuse. That she needed to stay with Olivia. That she had to talk to Meg right that minute. That she needed to go to the bathroom immediately.

Instead, she'd given in to the temptation to be with him.

She needed to be stronger when it came to Hunter Buchanan.

After the gun advertisement earlier and her conversation with her attorney, it had taken her a long time to settle down. By the time she pulled it together and finished getting ready, it had been peak car service time and she'd needed to wait twenty minutes for her driver to show up. She hadn't wanted to drive, though, because she'd expected that she'd be staying late and drinking.

Or maybe she was too shaken up to drive.

Either way, it had meant she had been late for the party. Then again, maybe walking into a get-together already in full swing was easier. Because if Meg got a good look at her face, she'd figure out in two seconds that something was wrong.

Except Meg's brother was probably as perceptive. Maybe more so. He seemed to notice things about her that she hid carefully.

"How's training going?" she asked, staring out at the yard, not wanting to make eye contact. She ducked away from the house, taking a seat on one of the deck chairs farthest from the light. Maybe if she could keep her face hidden, he wouldn't see how upset she was.

"It's good." He tucked a hand in his pocket, holding his beer bottle against his side in the other. "Top of my class, Meg said."

"That's wonderful, Hunter." Her genuine happiness for him pushed aside the anxiety she'd been carrying around since the gun advertisement had showed up in her home. "You've worked so hard. I'm so happy for you."

"Thank you." He grinned. "I wouldn't have been able to do it without you."

She turned her champagne flute in her hands, uncomfortable with the praise. "Leslie did the heavy lifting. I just helped at the end, to take the credit." She shrugged, unable to meet his eyes.

"No, not the rehab. I meant the jumps. Thank you for going with me. You have no idea how much that helped me."

Except she did. She'd been able to see it on his face, first for the bungee jump and then for the parachute. "You're welcome."

He sat down in the chair adjacent to her, placing his empty bottle on the table nearby. He folded his hands in front of him, staring at them. With a sigh, he added in a softer voice, almost as a confession, "I'm doing well, but it's not exactly like I expected it would be."

Cocking her head, she didn't bother to hide her surprise. "What do you mean? You told me that this was what had driven you the past year." He might have alluded to how much it meant to him, but his sister had been more forthcoming. Meg had mentioned that getting to training this year had been the driving force behind his recovery. She said she'd never seen someone so hell-bent on proving that he could be the same again.

"It was. I kept thinking that if I could finish training, that maybe it would undo everything that had happened last year. That I'd be able to put everything behind me, finally move on." He folded his hands, leaning his elbows on his knees. "It hasn't been like that, though."

His disappointment squeezed her chest. "No? What has it been like?"

"It's been a letdown." His blue eyes found her and his grin was sad. She wanted to reach for his hand, to touch him, but that would be stupid. She wouldn't want to stop at one touch. So she remained still, allowing him to go on. "I thought it would be the answer to everything. Now I'm just looking forward to a summer of waiting to jump out of an airplane and swing an ax or whatever."

"It's important work, Hunter. Heroic work. You save lives and property. You save the forests. It's important." Did she need to convince him? If Hunter couldn't see how much good smokejumpers did, she wasn't sure there was any impressing him.

"I know. It needs to be done. And I can do it, I've proved that already. I'm physically able to do it now, after all this time." He shook his head. "I'm just not sure I want to."

She could only stare at him. She suspected that he'd never told that to anyone. Why? He had friends, family who loved him. Why hadn't he told them he was questioning his decisions? And if he couldn't tell them, why was he telling her?

The answers to all of those questions were probably as dangerous as the questions themselves, so she attempted to deflect, leave them alone. "You know, maybe it's that you built up an expectation. If you were using training as a carrot, something to motivate you to get better, then maybe you built it up in your head."

"Maybe." He sighed.

She should let it go. He wasn't hers to worry about, to help. But she couldn't. Because he mattered to her.

She reached over and squeezed his forearm. "Hey, if you aren't happy, it's okay. Even if you decide that smokejumping isn't the long-term job for you, that's fine, too. Honestly, if it got you through the last year of pain and recovery, then it was worth it, no matter what it ends up being to your life."

He held her gaze and remained completely still. She was insanely aware of the contact where she touched him. He probably was, too.

As the moment lengthened, she remembered their kiss, and her eyes strayed to his mouth. God, his lips. She'd tried to forget exactly how amazing it had been to kiss him. During the day, she'd been able to distract herself, but at night, she lay awake, wondering if he thought about her, too.

"Charlie, please stop."

Her eyes lifted to his, her face heating. Except she didn't find teasing there. If anything, the naked want on his features warmed the rest of her. Flexing, her fingers tightened into his arm for a moment before she released him. "I'm so sorry."

His gaze lifted to the stars and he leaned back, exhaling with a laugh. "What the hell are you sorry about? I only mean stop because I don't think you actually want me to kiss you again. At least, your head doesn't."

She swallowed, because he had it exactly right. Her logical mind said kissing Hunter Buchanan was a bad idea. The first kiss had been enough to keep her distracted and aching for the past few weeks. She'd told herself it wouldn't happen again, that she needed to forget all about it. For his sake and hers. He didn't deserve her messing with his emotions.

"I'm sorry."

"God, Charlie. I'm not. I want you." His eyes burned into hers, scorching her. "I'm not going to pretend I don't. That kiss? I loved it. Every time I think about it, I want to do it again. Not only because of me, but because of the way you reacted. The way you breathed, the way you felt against me. The way you pulled me closer. I want that all again. But if I don't ever get that again, I'm a big boy. I can definitely manage my own wants and desires." His lips tilted. "Doesn't mean I'll stop wanting and desiring. But you don't have to feel sorry about it. It's a compliment."

She exhaled a breathy laugh. Everything he said should have made her uncomfortable. Instead, she burned. "Then, thank you."

"You're welcome." He leaned closer, rocking forward. "And, I think you want me, too."

She looked away quickly. Because she did. God, she did. "Hunter, I—"

"I'm not saying that to put you on the spot or to try to change your mind. I'm saying it because I'm guessing that there's something going on with you, something that's stopping you. Which is completely your prerogative. You don't talk about yourself and you're keeping me away, even though I think you don't want to. I might be wrong, but I think you're hiding." He offered her a sad smile. "But if you ever want to stop, you let me know, okay? Because I'd love to know you better."

She could only nod. What she wanted was to open up to him, to tell him about the advertisement she had received today. To tell him about Joshua.

Could she trust him? In all of her relationships she'd made the mistake of falling too fast, trusting too soon. Each time, she'd been let down or used, culminating in what had happened in Chicago with Joshua, forcing her to run across the country to avoid him.

She couldn't afford to go through that again. She didn't think her heart could take it.

Suddenly, it was all too much. Beyond the sliding doors, her friend was still surrounded by people who were happy for her, all celebrating the bright future Meg and Lance would have.

With a threatening message on her kitchen table at home and a man she couldn't open up to beside her, that kind of happiness seemed completely out of her reach.

"I think I'm going to get going." She pulled her phone out of her handbag, opening a ride-hailing app. Damn it, another half an hour wait. She should have driven. She'd had one drink.

"Sure." He got to his feet. "Don't request a car. I can drive you home."

She glanced up at him. "Don't you want to stay? Be with Meg?"

He offered her his hand. "I'm supposed to see them tomorrow, help them clean up. Besides, I knew about the engagement. I've congratulated them both already."

"Are you sure?" She didn't want to put him out, but she couldn't be here with everyone right now.

"Absolutely. It's been a long week. I'm tired, too."

She had no idea if he was actually ready to leave or if he was only saying that so he could drive her, but she didn't feel like waiting for the car service. Standing, she collected her empty champagne glass. "Thanks. I'd appreciate that. I just need to say congratulations to Meg."

As Hunter's hand found the small of her back, comfort spread through her, like it always did when he was around. She wanted to lean back into it, to let him be there for her.

Instead, she straightened, her throat tight, and went in search of her friend.

Chapter Eleven

He'd been too straightforward with her.

As Hunter drove the short distance to Charlie's apartment, he couldn't figure out a way to break the silence. Instinctively, he guessed that anything less than complete honesty wouldn't work with her. She was already as skittish as a cat.

Except the truth hadn't helped him either.

Maybe there was no way to get through to her. If she wasn't willing to take a chance on him, there wasn't much he could do to convince her otherwise. Which sucked. But it was completely her call.

When he pulled in front of the house where she had an apartment, he turned off the engine, opening his door.

"Hunter, you don't have to—"

"Door-to-door service, my lady," he said, trying to keep things light. She grinned back, but she looked as exhausted as he felt.

She climbed out, and he followed her up the sidewalk.

Except when she reached the stairs, she paused. "I know I locked that."

Stepping beside her, he noticed her door was ajar. "You're sure?"

"Yeah. After what happened today? Yes." She bounded up the stairs, reaching for the doorknob when he stopped her.

Wait. What happened today? What was she talking about?

He reached for her arm, pulling her to a stop. "Absolutely not. You aren't going in there. We're calling the police. Are you sure no one else could be in there?" He resisted his desire to push her behind him even as he tugged her hand, drawing her away.

Shaking her head, she swallowed. "No. No one else lives with me."

He pressed the unlock button on his SUV. "Into the car, then." He didn't watch her go, only stared at that door as if it were a snake that might strike. "Please."

As he backed away too, his heart thudded in his ears, his fingers tightening around his phone. But he didn't look down to call the cops until he heard the door close on the TrailBlazer. Then, still backing away, he dialed 911. When they asked what his emergency was, he said, "We think there's been a break-in."

Admirably, it took the Bend police less than five minutes to arrive. When they did, he pointed them toward the door and a pair of officers went in, their weapons ready.

They returned minutes later, shaking their heads.

Nothing.

Hunter and Charlie got out of the TrailBlazer as one of the officers approached, the other returning to the police car. "You Hunter Buchanan?"

Stretching out his hand, he nodded. "Yes. This is Charlie Jones, though. She lives here."

"There's no one inside now, ma'am," the officer said. "But they've done a real number on your place. We can escort you in, if you'd like. See if there's anything missing immediately, but I would like to ask a few more questions after my partner finishes calling this in."

Charlie nodded, not saying anything as she wrapped her arms around her stomach, heading up the stairs. Hunter followed her, because at a time like this, he didn't want to leave her alone.

Inside, all of the lights were on. The brightness threw the mess into stark reality. Everything had been ripped up. Books thrown off the shelves, papers emptied onto the floor. Lamps were on the ground, broken. Pictures were either crooked or off the walls entirely. In the kitchen, the refrigerator had been ransacked, food scattered everywhere. Shards of glass from broken dishes crunched under Charlie's feet.

But while the state of the place was shocking, her lack of reaction surprised him the most. "Charlie?"

She trailed a finger along her counter. "Yeah?"

Asking if she was okay would be pointless. Though his first instinct was to touch her, to hold her hand, he didn't. She seemed fragile. "I just wanted you to know I'm here."

When her eyes lifted and her gaze met his, the brokenness he found there squeezed his stomach. "Thanks. I appreciate it." She scanned the room again, sighing shakily. "I need to go talk with the police."

He let her go ahead of him, following her out of the ransacked house. As she reached the police cruiser, the cop—Officer Randall—nodded. "Did you see anything missing?"

"My computer was still there. I can't be sure if there is anything else missing, though, with all the mess." She swallowed. "I'll need to look more closely. Later."

"Of course." Randall motioned to the car. "Did you want to talk here or at the precinct?"

"Here, please." She shook her head, inhaling as if to steady herself. "My real name is Charlotte Michaelson, though I changed my name legally to Charlotte Jones a few years ago. I moved here three years ago from Chicago after I helped put an abusive man behind bars. His name is Joshua Oldham. I'm afraid that he's found me."

Shock raced through Hunter. Nothing had prepared him for this. Meg had said she was private, and he'd noticed she didn't talk about herself. God, tonight he'd even called her out for hiding from him. He might have suspected some pain in her past—an old flame, a bad experience—but this was beyond his imagination.

"Oh, okay." Officer Randall jotted down some notes. "You know what? Are you sure you wouldn't like to go to the precinct? I'll have more resources at my fingertips, to look things up, to take notes. If this isn't a random break-in, we should have you talk down there."

She nodded quickly. "Sure. Oh, but hang on a minute." She dashed back into the apartment. When she returned, she was holding a piece of paper. "You're going to need this."

"What is this, ma'am?"

"I received that in the mail earlier."

In the streetlight, Hunter made out what looked to be a page from a magazine. On it was an advertisement for a pistol.

* * * *

Two hours later, Charlie joined Hunter in the police department waiting room. The place was clean, but it had an institutionalized feel. Nothing matched, a mishmash of army green, checkerboard linoleum floors, and walls that screamed for a coat of paint. She'd told Hunter that she could get a car home when she was done, but he'd insisted on waiting. Truth be told, she hadn't pushed too hard. She hadn't wanted to ride home to her ransacked apartment alone. It would be nice to go back there with a friend.

Which was what he'd proved himself to be this evening.

Earlier, Officer Randall had offered to drive her to the station. She'd tried to say goodbye to Hunter there. He'd wanted nothing of it, insisting she'd need someone to drive her home later.

She'd let him. Just like she'd let him sit in the waiting room for two hours while she answered a million questions, aware that he probably had that many as well.

It was well past ten o'clock. He'd looked tired at Meg's party, and the dark smudges under his eyes were even more pronounced now. He'd spent the past three weeks doing some of the most physically demanding training out there. He must be dead on his feet.

Still, he'd waited for her.

"Are you ready to go?" His brow lifted.

God, he killed her. Anyone else's expression would be full of questions, even frustration at being left to wait for so long with no explanation. But him? He only looked concerned.

For her.

She wanted to fall into his arms, to let his warm and strong body hold her up. Instead, she folded her arms around her. "Yes. I'm done."

He nodded. "Did you want me to take you home? Or is there somewhere else you can go for the night?"

She'd considered this. Sleeping in her place in its current state would be impossible. What else was she going to do, though? She had no family in Oregon. She refused to bother Meg and Lance when they probably hadn't even finished the party celebrating their engagement. She could call Olivia, but she'd seen her at Meg's, already a few cocktails in and eyeing one of the smokejumpers on Lance's team. Maybe Leslie…

But she didn't want to face Leslie right now. It would mean she'd need to address Leslie's offer. So soon after the break-in, she couldn't see a time in the future when she would feel safe enough to consider settling down here or anywhere.

Oh well. If she couldn't sleep, she could start cleaning up. The police said they would drive by her house more often, keep track of her. Tomorrow, she'd call the landlord about having a security system installed.

For now, though, she might need to accept that sleep wasn't in her future.

"I don't have family. I'm good. I need to start cleaning up anyway." She smiled, attempting to convince him that she was fine. Because the concern on his face was too tempting. She could lean on this man, let him help her. She wanted to. But tonight, with everything that had happened, she didn't trust herself.

The questions had gone on forever. Having to rehash everything she'd wanted to forget all those years ago? It had been difficult.

Mostly, it had been a long day. She could use the chance to go home and lick her wounds.

Except his face said otherwise.

"You don't have anyone else." He scowled. "I'm not leaving you to be by yourself tonight."

"You definitely don't have to do that." Right now, she couldn't decide if she wanted him to stay or go. Everything was too raw.

His eyes searched her face. She didn't shy away, instinctively sensing that she didn't need to run from him. He understood, somehow. Maybe it was that he'd been through so much himself. He'd come back from injuries that could have killed him. He'd probably wondered why it had happened to him, what was the matter with the universe that it had chosen him for that kind of suffering.

She could relate. Maybe that was why they got each other. They'd been through things that couldn't be explained to other people.

He covered her hand with his. "Charlie, it's fine. I get it. I just know that there were times people left me alone because they thought I needed to be by myself but what I needed was for someone to be there."

Her eyes stung. She blinked hard, refusing to cry here, in front of him. She'd made it through the police questioning. She'd walked through the place she'd started to think of as her home without losing her cool. She couldn't lose it now, under his sympathetic gaze.

"Come to my place," he said. "No expectations. Just come and be there. Tomorrow morning I'll drive you home and you can face everything then, in the daylight. But tonight, come home with me."

"Yes," she answered, before she could give herself time to overthink. "Yes."

He nodded. Still holding her hand, he removed it from his forearm and tucked it in the crook of his arm as he escorted her out to his TrailBlazer.

When he got in, he turned the heat on. It wasn't cold outside, though, so she crinkled her nose in question at him.

"Your fingers are cold." He started the car and they headed toward Redmond.

He didn't say anything during the drive. Maybe it was his lack of pushiness that made her want to talk, because she found herself opening up the conversation.

"You must have questions." He had to. The entire evening had been one confusing revelation after another. She had changed her name. She was in hiding. She'd been getting threatening notes. And that was only the stuff he knew about.

He didn't even know the whole story.

"Of course. But I figured you'd tell me what you want to tell me." He glanced at her before returning his gaze to the road. "You never asked me a million prying questions about my accident."

And at that moment, she realized she was in serious danger of falling hard for him.

She might not know him very well. But Hunter Buchanan was so incredibly decent and he'd been through so much. More, though, he respected her. He understood her. She didn't understand how, but she recognized it, somewhere very fundamental.

Which was what made her say, "I ran away. From Chicago."

He didn't respond.

"I ended up there to finish college after two years of community college in Ohio. Northwestern, for physical therapy. When I graduated, I wanted to stay. I'd spent most of my childhood moving with my parents. We never stayed in one place. They liked to travel, try new things. Different countries. I did a year in Buenos Aires, another in Bali. All over the US. They're in the Southwest now, but who knows for how long." She chuckled. "I wanted to stay somewhere longer, to actually live in one place for more than a year."

Those couple of years after college had been magical. It had been her first experience making friends she intended to keep. She'd lived in a walk-up with two of her sorority sisters. She'd spent those years eating horribly and drinking too much.

"I met Joshua at the first job I had after graduation." Staring out the window, the scenery blurred as she became lost in her memories. "It was one of three branches of the same physical therapy firm, all owned by him. He was young, motivated, handsome." She shook her head. "He was incredibly charming. Though I was sure that going out with my boss was a bad idea, I was young and overwhelmed. What came next was a whirlwind month."

Even now, trying to explain, it sounded stupid. Obviously going out with the owner of your company would be a bad move. She'd realized that back then. Her sorority sisters had warned her, told her to tread carefully.

She hadn't listened. It had all seemed so romantic.

"I found out a month in that he was engaged and also pursuing another girl in another branch. When I told him I wanted to end it, he threatened my job." She shrugged. "I spoke with an attorney. But it wasn't until I talked to the girl in the other branch that things got weird."

She glanced out the window. "Apparently, word traveled fast. She'd confronted him and told his fiancée. He was livid." She closed her eyes. "When I saw her, she had a broken arm and a black eye."

When Kelly had invited her over, she'd worried that visiting was a bad idea. She hadn't wanted to fall into any sort of drama. As far as she'd been concerned, Joshua had proved he was a cheater and not worth her time. She had only wanted to get back to doing her job and pretend none of it had ever happened.

"The other girl—Kelly—had said that he'd gotten mad when his fiancée found out and left him. He said that though he'd lost her, he refused to lose either of us." Charlie snorted. "I hadn't believed her at first. He'd never seemed like the violent sort. I asked if she had struck out at him, what she'd done to threaten him first." She glanced at the ceiling of the car, as if she'd find understanding from the heavens above. "Later, I was so ashamed of myself for blaming the victim. I just couldn't believe it. Joshua didn't seem like he would ever do something like that."

"Until he came for you." Hunter's voice was controlled, but his fingers were tight on the steering wheel as he stared ahead at the light of the headlights.

She wondered what he was thinking. The next part was hard. She'd only confided in her parents and a friend she'd gone to in Chicago. "Yes."

He exhaled, and she hurried on, wanting to get it all out. "Kelly got it worse than I did. After we talked, I bought pepper spray. When he followed me home one night, he only hit me twice before I got him with it, called the police." Still, the memory of those two blows lived on, even years later. "He didn't do any permanent damage." He'd hit her in the cheek, punched her in the ribs. One of the bones there had cracked, but it had healed.

"Where did he hit you?"

She sighed. He didn't need the details, did he? "I healed, Hunter."

"Where?" His voice was low, broken.

"My face"—she patted her cheek—"and my ribs." She touched her left side, low, briefly remembering the pain. Then she returned her hands to her lap. "I made out better than Kelly. Her cheekbone was—"

"Stop, please." He pulled over to the side of the road. His hands still on the steering wheel, he dropped his chin to his chest and exhaled slowly.

She reached for him, placing her hand on his arm. "Hunter?" She shouldn't have said anything. She'd upset him. It wasn't pleasant conversation, but it was part of the story and he'd asked to know what happened. "I'm sorry."

"Why are you apologizing?" He tilted his head to her.

"I don't know. You're upset." She shrugged.

"Not because of you. You didn't do anything." He shifted, taking her hands in his. "Some asshole thought he could lift his hand to you, hurt you, because he didn't get what he wanted. Like a toddler in a sandbox. Men like that, they aren't men. I have a mother and a sister, women I love more than anything. If someone tried to hurt them, I'd want to rip their face off." His gaze met hers in the dim streetlights. "And because he hurt you, I feel the same."

She rubbed her fingers over his, swallowing. "It was years ago. I healed. And, well, I convinced Kelly and his fiancée to come with me, press charges. He was convicted of aggravated assault, because of our injuries, and sentenced to five years." She remembered her relief sitting in the courtroom, watching the verdict being handed down. It had felt like justice, for all of them. "I didn't stay, though. Right after that, I moved twice. First, to Denver. But the job there wasn't a good fit. So I came here."

Her friends and attorney in Chicago hadn't understood. Joshua had been in jail. She was safe, they told her. But that hadn't helped her sleep at night.

More, it had removed the joy of setting roots down there. She'd decided to find somewhere else. When she had arrived in Oregon, she'd changed her name.

"I hope he's spending his time in jail learning how to treat people," Hunter growled.

"He must have. Because when I spoke with my attorney this evening, she told me that he'd been released early, a few months ago." She smiled sadly. "For good behavior."

Chapter Twelve

Turning off the car outside his duplex in Redmond, Hunter scanned the shadows. Nothing, as usual. He lived in a quiet part of town, so he hadn't expected anything. But he tried to see it all through Charlie's eyes. He wanted her to feel comfortable here. Safe.

He pushed the front door open, letting Charlie go ahead of him. Closing it, he made sure to lock the deadbolt and latch the chain, something he didn't always do when he was here alone. As he left her in the foyer, he turned on the lights in the living room and the one in the kitchen.

Around him, he surveyed the stark minimalism of his place. Compared to her cozy, almost bohemian-looking one-bedroom, his place looked especially barren. He shrugged at her, sheepish. "It's not much, but I'm not here often."

"It's great. Thanks for having me."

Standing there, she pretended she was solid. Her smile was brave and genuine. Except her skin was pale, paler than usual. When he'd held her hands, they were icy. The smudges under her eyes were dark, a testament to the stressful situation.

What got him in the gut was that she probably didn't realize how shaken up she was. As she was telling him her story in the car, it had been like she was reciting details from someone else's life or a movie she'd watched. When he'd gotten upset, had to pull over because he could barely see through his fury for her, she'd reached for him, checked in on him.

She'd apologized for upsetting him.

Christ.

Even now, he had to take a deep breath. She didn't need any of that from him. Right now, he had to focus on what he could do for her.

"What can I get you?" he asked. *"Mi casa, su casa."*

She grinned, gripping her handbag in front of her and stepping further inside. "Actually, I was wondering if it would be too much to ask to use your shower."

"Right this way."

He showed her into the bathroom, instructed her how to use the faucet in the tub. It was touchy. Place was a rental, though, so he'd learned to deal with the foibles. He got her his fluffiest towel, his softest T-shirt, and his smallest pair of shorts.

When she surfaced after her shower, swallowed up by his clothes, her hair a mass of curls around her face, he had to stifle his groan. He'd always liked those clothes, but she made them look amazing.

To distract himself, he pushed a mug toward her. "You drink whiskey?"

"I have drunk whiskey in my past." She eyed the cup skeptically. "Do I drink it regularly? No."

"Hot toddy." He wiped the counter, disposing of the tea bag he'd used. "My mom's recipe for all things that ail you."

She glanced in the mug. "What is it?"

"Tea." He lifted the box of herbal tea he'd used. "I only have decaf since I only drink tea at night."

"You drink tea?"

"What's that face?" He covered his heart, feigning offense. "Lots of people drink tea."

"I drink tea." She lifted her shoulder. "I just didn't take you for a tea drinker."

"That's super judgy. Just goes to show there's a lot you don't know about me." He pushed the mug closer to her. "So it's tea and whiskey with a little lemon and honey. Mom puts a cinnamon stick in it, but I don't have those. Try it. Or don't. It's up to you." He hadn't been able to sit still while she'd showered, torn between thinking about her naked in there and worrying about how she was doing. He lifted his own mug, taking a sip. "Made myself one, too."

She took a sip and grinned. "Hey, it's good."

"Now I'm really offended. Of course it's good."

She laughed, and the sound warmed him more than the drink. He had wanted to relax her, to make her smile. To make her forget what had happened tonight. Or if not forget, at least not focus on it. She could deal with reality and be strong in the morning. Right now, she was here, with him. And he planned to take care of her.

"So what other hidden talents do you have?" she teased.

"Nothing hidden, honestly." He lifted his hands. "You hungry?"

"Um, kind of?" She narrowed her eyes, having a seat on one of the barstools. "Is this where you tell me that you're a four-star chef, too?"

"That's a question I will answer another time." He pointed at her. "But, for you, at midnight, after a shocking experience, I have something better than fancy food." He reached into the cabinet next to the stove and pulled out a paper bag covered in plastic wrap. "Microwave popcorn."

"You are a hero."

Less than five minutes later, they were munching. Hunter cast a surreptitious glance at Charlie's mug. Empty.

Good.

As she reached into the popcorn bowl, her cheeks had more color to them. Her mouth wasn't as tight.

Still looked tired, though.

He pushed the bowl toward her, watching her scoop the last handful out like a pro. There was, after all, only one right way to eat popcorn: by the overflowing handful, shoved directly in your mouth.

As she picked around the last kernels, trying to nab the rest of the pieces, he washed his hands. "How are you feeling?"

"Good." She grinned, reaching for a napkin. "Sleepy."

To prove her point, she yawned.

Whisking the bowl into the sink, he came around the counter in his postage-stamp kitchen and helped her off the barstool. "Come on, lady. Off to bed."

As he guided her down the hall, she put on the brakes. "Wait. I'm not sleeping in your room."

He was sure his expression said she was losing it. Because that's what he thought. "Where the hell else are you going to sleep?"

"On the couch." She backed away from his bedroom. "Like a normal guest."

"You are absolutely not sleeping on my couch."

"I can't sleep in your bed."

He placed one hand at the small of her back and the other on her elbow, ushering her toward his room. "I don't have my other sheets clean, because I just changed the sheets a couple days ago. So, sorry about that. But they should be fine."

"That's not what I meant." She stopped, and short of picking her up, he wasn't going to move her. He could only scowl down at her. "You're being nice enough to let me stay. I can't take your bed. You're tired, too."

"I know we don't know each other that well, but I swear to you that I wouldn't be able to sleep here with you on the couch." Yeah, because his mother would haunt his dreams, ragging on him about manners and chivalry.

But more than that, she was the one who'd had the scare. She was the one who was shaken up, who needed the rest. And he was hell-bent on her getting it.

"Besides," he offered, "I fall asleep watching television on the couch all the time. It's not a big deal."

Whatever he'd said, it must have gotten through to her. Or she was so tired that she didn't want to fight with him anymore. Either way, she let him guide her into his room and turn down the sheets.

Some people didn't make their beds regularly, but he wasn't those people. He preferred to climb into crisp, tidy sheets. It was a thing.

She pointed to the bathroom, blushing, and as she hurried off, he glanced toward the ceiling, praying for deliverance. Because Charlie Jones, in his clothes, with a fresh face and wearing a blush, was pretty much the hottest thing he'd ever seen.

When she returned, though, he'd organized his face in a respectable way. He gave her the remote to the TV. "Anything else you need to sleep?"

"I'm good."

He nodded, retreating, pulling the door closed behind him.

"Hey, Hunt?" she called.

He pushed the door open again, peeking his head in and trying to ignore his body's response to this woman, tucked in his bed. "Yeah?"

"Could you, maybe, leave the door open?"

Swallowing around the lump in his throat, he touched his eyebrow, saluting her. "Absolutely. Come and get me if you need anything."

She nodded, pulling his comforter up to her chin, her eyelids already droopy. Definitely exhausted. Trauma did that to a person.

He forced himself to head to the bathroom, brush his teeth, and then return to the living room. As he stretched out on the couch, he took some deep breaths and attempted to think of his family, work, anything to get his mind off of her.

But that only allowed the anger about her asshole former boss to run loose in his brain.

His Charlie had changed her name to feel safe from that guy. She'd come here, switched her name, and tried to settle in.

Now the bastard was free.

Could what was happening with her tonight have to do with that dickhead? Was that guy stalking Charlie?

If someone was searching for Charlie, then they'd need to go through him first. If she needed to stay here, at his place, he'd let her know she was welcome.

Except she wouldn't, would she? He'd only started to really get to know her over the past month or so, but she wasn't going to lean on him, even if he asked. She was strong, would insist on doing things herself.

He shifted on the couch, grabbing the throw blanket and tucking it around himself, and turned on his side. He punched his pillow before sliding his arm under his head. He couldn't get comfortable, thinking of some guy threatening her.

His heart rate picked up, and he recognized them: the beginning phases of a panic attack. He tried to regulate his breathing, slow his pulse.

"Hunter?"

He rolled to see her, standing in the hall in front of his room. She looked miniature in his clothes, and her eyes were wide as quarters. "Yeah?"

"So, would it be okay if I just hang out here with you for a little while?" She stepped closer, motioned to the chair. "Maybe watch TV or something?"

If it was anyone else, he probably wouldn't have thought anything of it. But Charlie? She didn't shift her weight like that. Her voice didn't break the slightest bit, the way it had.

She didn't want to be alone.

"Sure. No worries." He sat up, throwing his blanket over the back of the couch, and got to his feet.

She lifted her hands. "Wait, what are you doing? I'll sit here, with you."

"Absolutely not." He reached her in a few steps, taking her hand. "We're going to hang out in my room, watch something there."

She narrowed her eyes at him. "Wait. We are? In there?"

"Fine," he said, still pulling her by the hand. "Not 'we.' I'm going to watch TV with you while you fall asleep."

In his room, she paused, staring at the bed. Her disorientation squeezed him again. "I'm sorry. I just can't, well, I don't want..." She inhaled and exhaled slowly. "Fine, I'm having a hard time being by myself."

"I know."

She crossed her arms over her chest. "You know?"

"Yes." He nodded, crawling onto the bed and patting the right side. The one he didn't sleep on. "If I'd gone through what you just went through, I wouldn't want to be alone either. Totally normal." He punched the pillow on that side, motioning her over. "Come on. This home network show is new, I think. Another program where they flip the houses. You watch this stuff?"

He'd wanted to lighten things up. She was uncomfortable in his place, afraid, anxious. He got it. He'd been there. But when she caught her lip between her teeth and her brow wrinkled, his stomach sank. He had a sister. He was familiar with what a woman looked like close to tears. "Aww Char, come here…"

She took two steps and jumped onto the bed next to him. Without making eye contact, she wiggled under the covers, pulling them over herself. Apparently she didn't want to talk about how upset she was anymore.

He stayed on top of the comforter, his ankles crossed, his arm tucked behind his head. The show he'd chosen was monotonous, like watching The Weather Channel or the jewelry network. He continued to cast glances at her, checking to see if she was drifting. Sure enough, her eyes were closed.

He'd slept with women before, even had some brief relationships. But he didn't think anything had ever been as intimate as lying next to Charlie, with all the covers between them, watching her fall asleep.

Then, her hand found his, squeezing. He swallowed, tightening his own fingers.

"Hunter?"

"Yeah," he whispered, barely recognizing his voice.

"You're planning to go back to the couch when I fall asleep, aren't you?"

"Yeah." It would be for the best, to put a room of distance between them.

"Don't." Her eyes opened, finding his. "Stay here, with me. Tonight." Her gaze searched his, and he saw her begin to regret asking. "I mean, if you want—"

"Stop. Of course I'll stay if you want me to. But is it okay if I get under the covers?" When she didn't immediately agree, he shook his head. "No biggie. I'm good here." He leaned down to grab the blanket at the foot of the bed.

"Yes." She tugged the covers down. "Climb in."

He didn't say much, only shifted between the sheets with her. But when she wiggled closer, pressing herself against him, he couldn't stifle his groan. His eyes closed, and he desperately attempted to get ahold of the wash of lust slicing through him even as he pulled her closer against him.

Except, as her curves settled against the planes of him, something different coursed through him. It was as if all the shapes and edges of him had been waiting to find the shapes and edges of her. He sighed, only to catch the scent of his shampoo in her hair.

He flipped off the television, and the darkness closed in around them. Offhand, he realized that the beginnings of his panic attack in the living room had never become full-blown.

In the quiet, with Charlie pressed against him, there was only peace.

Chapter Thirteen

When Charlie opened her eyes the next morning, she was warm. Next to her, the curtains blocked most of the light, but around the borders, it streamed in.

Except those weren't her curtains.

Scanning the sparse room, her gaze landed on the man sprawled next to her. Hunter.

The events of last night replayed in her mind. Her apartment had been wrecked. She'd had to speak with the police—about Joshua and the restraining order, about hiding in Oregon and changing her name. Then Hunter had brought her here, let her crash for the night.

She'd invited him to sleep in the bed with her. And it had been great.

More than anything, he'd been great. She wasn't sure if his experiences over the past few years had made him empathetic or if he was naturally understanding, but whatever it was, he got her.

Now, though, in the light of day, she had a hard time pretending.

They weren't only friends. She'd been afraid she'd fall for him, but who did she think she was kidding? She'd fallen already.

Hunter was an easy man to love.

She closed her eyes. Looking back on the weeks she'd gotten to know him, she should have seen how useless it would be.

She'd never been able to shield her heart. She'd been raised to live in the moment. Caution wasn't who she was.

Except after Joshua, she'd begun to second-guess herself. She'd doubted her heart, assumed that the problems she'd had with men were problems with her. She opened up too fast, gave too much of herself too quickly. Always had. After all, that's what she knew. Her parents were this shining example of openness and selflessness in a relationship. They might have a weird, bohemian life, flitting all over the country, but they loved each other.

She wanted that. She had been so eager to find it that she'd looked past flaws that she shouldn't have.

Was she doing that with Hunter? He was here for her in a time when she needed support. Last night, he'd stepped in as a knight in shining armor. Was he really that good, or was she not being careful enough?

As she rolled off the bed and headed for the bathroom, she grabbed the new, spare toothbrush he'd left for her last night. After she used the facilities and brushed her teeth, she stood in front of the mirror, staring herself down and letting everything swim in her head.

What she was left with was the recognition that it didn't matter if he was who he appeared to be or not. Because she was still the person that she was. And she had already fallen for him.

If that was the case, then why was she holding herself back? She wasn't ashamed of who she was. She was the kind of person who gave her all when she cared about someone. If things ended badly later, if her foolish heart had fallen wrong again, would she be any less hurt?

No, but she'd always regret not taking a chance on him now.

Nodding at the wild-haired, wild-eyed woman in front of her, she smiled, turned off the light, and returned to Hunter's room. She must have woken him, though, because the room was empty. She straightened the covers and went in search of him.

In the kitchen, he shut the lid on the coffeepot, turning to grin at her. "That's not decaf. You're welcome."

His sandy hair was disheveled, and whiskers had erupted on his jaw. In his T-shirt and pajama pants, he was so sexy he stole her breath.

As she stood there, staring at him, his grin disappeared. "If you don't want coffee here, though, no biggie. Just hang on, let me get dressed and I'll drive you home." He nodded and then headed for the bathroom. He'd closed the door before she could recover.

What had happened?

When he resurfaced a few minutes later, his hair was tamed. "Give me a second," he said. "I'll put on some pants." He shuffled into the bedroom, reaching for a dresser drawer.

"Hunter?" She stepped inside, her heart pounding in her ears. "Wait."

He straightened from where he'd begun riffling through the drawer, his brow creased. She stepped forward, gazing up at him. "Could I kiss you, please?"

He stilled and then searched her face for a split second before he reached for her, his hands cupping her face and his mouth falling on hers.

Her eyes widened and then closed as his lips consumed her. She sighed, shifting closer, her hands bunching into the fabric at his waist and pulling him into her. The hunger in him sang through her body, settling in her stomach. She shook with need—to taste him, to breathe him in, to get as close as she could.

Last night, he'd grounded her. At first, she'd lain in his bed, with him in the living room, and she'd been unable to settle. She kept thinking about her apartment, about how torn up it was. But mostly, she'd been completely alone in that unfamiliar bed that smelled like him. All she could be sure of was that she wanted to be with him.

When they'd curled up next to each other, she'd figured it out. Every time she'd fallen into his arms had felt like home.

For a girl who hadn't ever had a true home, that was saying something. She hadn't recognized it for what it was during their first kiss, but she had the night before.

Home.

Now she got that same contentment, but it mixed with the pounding ache inside her. Their kisses became more desperate, and she pressed into him, coaxing him backward until he sat on the bed. She followed him down, straddling his lap. From this angle, she was higher, so she buried her hands in his soft hair and pulled him toward her. This way, she could control the kiss—and she did, angling her mouth over his again and again.

He ran his hands up her back, settling them at her shoulder blades. He didn't exert any pressure, but the way he held her was reverent.

Soon, kisses weren't enough. Dropping her hands from his hair, she pulled the soft T-shirt he'd given her to wear over her head. She hadn't bothered to get back into her bra and underwear after her shower. All her clothes had felt dirty.

She sat astride him in the morning light, topless.

His gaze roamed over her, and she warmed in his heat. When she expected him to reach for her, though, he pulled at his own shirt, removing it. The wide expanse of his chest stole her bravado.

Every inch of him was tanned and chiseled. Even with him seated, she could make out the defined shape of his abdominal muscles. She'd worked out with him, gone jumping off a bridge with him. Hell, she'd kissed him, her entire front pressed against him. So she'd been aware that he was cut and gorgeous. But this?

Everything about his shape appealed to her, made even more sexy because he didn't seem at all cocky about it. He only watched her as she looked at him. She ran her fingers along his collarbone. His pulse beat quickly when she moved over his neck. Then she trailed down his sternum, to those ab muscles. When he sucked in a quick breath, she retrieved her hand.

As their gazes connected, she wondered why he wasn't touching her, too. So she lifted his left hand and placed it over her breast. As he covered her, he reached for her other breast with his free hand, his eyes finding hers in question.

"Yes," she sighed, and he didn't need any other encouragement. Her eyes closed as he explored the curves of her, and she gasped. "More. Your mouth. Please."

When his warm breath feathered over her sensitive nipple, she opened her eyes, needing to watch. The sensation of his mouth covering her coupled with the view of this gorgeous man, completely engrossed in kissing her, made her cry out. His fingers moved to dig into her hips, but he didn't pull her closer, instead allowing her to press into his mouth on her own.

He must have figured out that she wanted to lead, because he was letting her take what she needed from him.

Antsy and overwhelmed by the desire racing through her, she got to her feet. The shorts he'd given her were big, and she'd had to roll them a few times to keep them from falling down. They didn't need more than a quick tug to fall off her hips, leaving her entirely naked in front of him.

Hunter's fingers dug into the comforter at the edge of the bed and he groaned. "God, Charlie. You're perfect."

His tone was so adoring that all of her earlier need to lead went out the window. What had she been trying to do? She wasn't the kind of girl to take pleasure with no consequences. Her heart was always in it. If she had been trying to prove that she was strong enough to weather sleeping with Hunter unscathed, she had been fooling herself.

She loved this man. Loving him would make her different, for better or worse. And no amount of being in charge in bed was going to change that.

As she stood, watching him, reeling in the emotions racing through her, his face changed. While the lust was still there, now there was also concern. "Are you okay? Do you want to stop?"

She shook her head. But she couldn't bring herself to move, too overwhelmed to speak.

Still holding her gaze, he stood, dropping his pants to the floor. Her gaze fell with them.

The bottom half of him was just as impressive as the top half. She ran her tongue along her bottom lip.

He groaned, and it turned into a chuckle as he held out his hand. "Wanna come in with me?" he asked, gesturing toward the bed.

She nodded. "Yes."

As he threw the comforter aside, she expected him to wave her in. Instead, he swept her up and placed her in the center of the mattress. The quick movement made her laugh, lifting the heaviness from what they were about to do. As she continued to giggle, he slipped in beside her, gathering her against him. "This okay?"

"Absolutely." God, all those muscles felt as good as they looked.

"What about if I run my fingers along your skin here?" He lifted up on one elbow, propping his head up so he could see her better, and pointed his other index finger to her breast.

"Yes," she whispered.

As he traced the outline of her, she gasped, her eyes closing as she gave herself over to the deliciousness of the feelings.

He paused, his fingers at her rib cage. "Charlie?" He waited until she opened her eyes again. "Is it okay if I touch your belly, here?" Again he pointed.

"Yes." Again the word was barely a breath. He nodded, his expression completely absorbed, and he continued his exploration.

When he finally reached the center of her, he said her name again, but it came out more of a plea than a question. Their eyes met, and she cupped his face in her hand.

"Sweetheart, can I touch you here?" he asked.

His fingers weren't moving, and the anticipation had her squirming against him, pressing up, desperate for him to keep going. "Oh God."

"That's not a yes," he said, his lip tilting up. But it did nothing to temper the emotion in his gaze.

"Please, God. Yes."

As his fingers dropped lower, finding the place where everything in her seemed to be centered, she gasped, jerking up and toward him.

Her orgasm crashed over her, so unexpected that she cried out with it. His strokes were masterful as he helped her to draw it out. When it was over, she was left lying in his arms, breathless.

"That definitely felt like a yes," he whispered, as he pushed the hair from her face and kissed her temple.

Then she was laughing, and she had no idea when in the course of their lovemaking it had gone from her wanting to be in charge to this, but she didn't care. "Will you please get inside me?"

He leaned over, dug around in the nightstand, and returned with a condom. In a quick moment, he had precautions taken care of and shifted to position himself between her thighs. Then he cupped her backside in his hands and pressed inside her.

She couldn't help what escaped her lips. It was half sigh, half moan, and all pleasure. She reached for him, needing to touch him, to hold him, too.

He pushed fully in and retreated, the friction making them both groan again. Then he leaned over her, pressed a kiss to her mouth and said, "Yes."

As Hunter began to move, she wrapped her legs around his waist and ran her hands along his sides. Her eyes drifted closed, and she lost herself in the movement and joy of the moment with him.

She tumbled over the edge again and he followed her, crying out. When they came down, she held him against her.

Who knew what the next days or weeks were going to bring? Someone had ransacked her home and she had no idea if her past had found her there, in Oregon. But right at that moment, she was thankful for whatever path had led her to him.

Chapter Fourteen

Hunter's stomach woke him up. As much as he liked lazing around in bed with Charlie, he was hungry and he bet she was, too. Time to feed them.

He patted her on the hip. "Up. We need food."

She grumbled, tucking her head back under the pillow, her bare ass still out of the covers and the arch of her graceful back on full display. He ran his fingers along her spine, wondering if he'd ever get enough of touching her. When she sighed, he damn near decided to ignore his hunger pains.

But if he was starving, so was she. A glance at the clock said it was nearly noon.

Food.

He shifted out of bed, pulling the covers over her until all he could see were a few dark curls peeking out. Snagging his pajama pants from the floor where he'd left them, he made a pit stop in the bathroom before heading into the kitchen.

Five minutes later, he'd started a new pot of coffee and had some bacon sizzling. When she appeared, pulling the T-shirt she'd worn earlier over her head and climbing onto a barstool, she rubbed her eyes. "That smells delicious."

He shrugged, grinning. "Of course it does. It's bacon." He pushed a mug of coffee toward her. "Cream, no sugar, right?" That's how she'd taken the cup she'd gotten last night, at the police department. He nudged the half-and-half over, and she poured.

After a sip, she sighed. "Thanks."

He nodded, winking at her over the rim of his own mug. "Not that I'm complaining, but feel like explaining what made you change your mind this morning?"

As he'd filled the coffeepot, he'd wondered if he should say anything about it. After all, a gorgeous and amazing woman had pretty much jumped his bones. Why complain? But this was Charlie. She wasn't like every other woman. She was special, and whatever was going on in her head mattered to him.

He cared about her. A few weeks ago, she'd basically told him that anything between them was a bad idea. That didn't explain this morning's bed gymnastics.

Color exploded on her cheeks, and she studied her coffee mug like the key to the universe was inside. He could have been right. Asking might have been a bad idea.

"I decided that I was done being afraid."

"Of me?" He set his cup on the counter, the coffee in his empty stomach turning to battery acid. "You were afraid of me?" He'd wondered if things with Joshua had scared her, made her hesitant around men. She'd never shied away or flinched when he approached her, though, so he hadn't been sure.

"No." She shook her head. "I was afraid of me."

He cocked his head, encouraging her to go on. She sighed, placing her mug in front of her and circling it between her palms. "Joshua wasn't the first guy I'd misjudged and thought was a better person than they were. There was Kevin and then Tyler in college, followed by Eddie right out of school. Joshua was just the worst." She grinned, but it was a sad grin. "They weren't all the same story, and I'll spare you the gory details, but things always fell apart. In the end I started wondering if maybe I'm just not a very good judge of character when it comes to men."

There wasn't anything he could say to her. He could run to her defense, insist that of course she was a good judge of character. But he was afraid it would come off like he was vouching for his own character. Considering that he'd been a mess this past year, he wasn't even sure he could do that. So he reached over and gripped her fingers..

She squeezed back. "Anyway, I reminded myself that wasn't who I was. I live in the moment. And, well, I wanted you." Again that blush that did strange things to his insides.

"I see." He did, kind of. Some of her explanation bothered him, though. What about last night had changed her mind? If seeing her place destroyed had changed her mind, he couldn't help but worry if she'd been thinking clearly. And wondering that she'd made a rash decision about him, or that she'd come to regret what they'd done, it didn't sit well with him.

To keep from letting her study his face, he returned to his bacon, removing it to a paper-towel-lined plate. What was nagging at him was that he wasn't sure he cared what had driven her into his arms. He'd loved having her there.

His biggest concern was that if something had driven her there in the first place, that same thing could drive her away just as fast.

As he pushed the plate of bacon in front of her, he cracked half a dozen eggs into a bowl, scrambled them up, and threw them into the pan with some of the bacon grease. He wasn't sure if it was a universally acknowledged fact, but eggs in bacon grease were the tastiest eggs out there.

They ate in silence, sipping coffee, and he'd like to think it was comfortable silence. But it wasn't.

When they finished and she walked around to put her plate in the sink, he snagged her arm. As their eyes met, he tried to smile. "That was awkward."

"Yeah, I know." Her brow furrowed. "What happened? You're not happy about how things went this morning?"

"Please." He snorted. "I loved everything about this morning. What I'm worried about is tomorrow morning."

"Tomorrow?"

"Yeah." He reached for her, cupping her face and letting his fingers trail into her hair. "Because if you changed your mind, I'm afraid you'll change it back. And I like having you around, Charlie Jones. A lot."

She wrapped her arms around him, and he dropped his mouth to cover hers.

He tried to put all of his emotions, everything coursing through him, into that kiss. He wanted it to say how much he had come to care for her, that he never wanted her to leave his side. That since he found whatever pulled them together, he couldn't imagine what it would feel like to have her missing.

But that would scare the shit out of her, he was certain.

So instead of saying all those words, he tried to allow his hands and his body to show her.

He tugged her shirt over her head, running his lips along every inch of her—her breasts, her collar, her neck, her face. Everything he could reach.

When the color was high on her face and her eyes were heavy, he swooped her up and carried her back to the still-unmade bed. Laying her down, he gave the shorts she was wearing a swift tug, and they came off her hips with ease.

Those shorts were definitely his new favorites.

Then he was touching all of her, his fingers trailing into the spaces that made her breathing hitch and her eyes drift closed.

When he crawled between her legs and dropped his mouth to the core of her, she cried out. The sound was musical, and its effect was like magic, coursing through his chest, his groin, his very soul. The taste of her sang through him, and he groaned against her, even as she writhed.

Reaching into the drawer next to his bed, he retrieved a condom and covered himself.

When he sank into her, her eyes shining up at him, he was sure he'd never felt such rightness. Though he wasn't the praying kind, he found himself offering up thanks to whatever twist of fate had sent this wandering girl into his life.

* * * *

"It's not him."

Charlie sat across from the investigator at Bend Police Department, her elbows on the table in the conference room. Or maybe it was an interrogation room. She wasn't sure what they called it, but there were a lot of empty chairs. Right now, they were the only people in the room along with all of her frustration.

The investigator—Vargas—had called her first thing this morning. Hunter had driven her to her apartment yesterday afternoon. They'd spent the day cleaning up, putting things in her place where they needed to go. They ordered pizza for dinner and watched a movie. When he'd stood to go, she'd stopped him. Call her a coward, but she hadn't wanted to spend the night alone.

Setting the place right had gone a long way to chasing away the nerves from returning. Before she returned, she hadn't been sure if she'd ever be able to look at her place the same again. While it used to be a safe haven, a place she was coming to see as a home, when she'd walked in, it had been as if she'd never lived there at all. Completely foreign.

But when things were righted, her pictures back on the wall, her drawers reorganized, she'd started to settle. With Hunter lying beside her last night, she'd been able to sleep.

"Are you absolutely certain?" She pressed her palm into the tabletop, rubbing her other hand through her hair. "You're sure that Joshua Oldham has no connection to the break-in at my house or the woman who pulled a gun on me on the street? The advertisement in the mail?"

It had to be him. There was nothing else.

The investigator's eyes were kind as he opened the file in front of him. "Here are records from his parole officer. He checks in regularly, even more than he's supposed to." He placed the piece of paper in front of her. "This is his course list at the seminary."

She pulled the list of classes toward her. "I'm sorry. Seminary?"

Vargas nodded. "He enrolled right out of prison." He smirked. "Found Jesus inside, apparently."

"He beat three women." She leaned back heavily in her seat. "Not all at once, but over a few days. He knew what he was doing."

"And now he's begging for your forgiveness." Detective Vargas lifted the final sheet from the file, placed it in front of her, and closed the folder. "Mr. Oldham wanted you to have this note."

She covered it with her hands and pushed it back toward him. "I don't want to read a thing he has to say." Absolutely not. There was nothing Joshua could say to her that was going to make what he'd done all right.

"Either way, there's no indication that he had anything to do with the events of the past month." Vargas patted the folder. "We're continuing our investigation, of course. But if you can think of anything that might help us, here's my card."

"Yes. Of course." She studied the paperwork in front of her. "Are you absolutely certain? There's no way he's involved?"

"I am." He shook his head. "He's been living at the seminary. They can vouch for his every move. I've checked the phone records, but he hasn't called hardly anyone since arriving. I'm continuing to check, to see if anyone he called or saw might have been acting for him. But there are no indications that's the case."

"I see." She nodded and then stood, gathering everything but the note. "Thank you so much."

"Miss Jones." Vargas had continued to call her by her current name instead of her old name. She appreciated it.

"Yes?" She paused at the door.

"Your note." He motioned to where she'd left Joshua's presumed apology. "You can choose to read it or not, but I'm not allowed to keep it."

She didn't want to argue, even though part of her wanted to tell this guy that he couldn't tell her what she wanted or didn't want. Instead, she picked up the slip of paper and added it to her pile before walking out of the room.

As she left the police department, her foreboding was worse than it had been when she had gone in. She'd expected to hear that Joshua was behind the addict, the letter, and the apartment break-in. She'd braced herself. To find out that it wasn't him, that whoever was responsible was still at large and anonymous? Well, turned out that was even worse.

Over the past three years, she'd made decisions because of him.

Her whole life had been about staying hidden from him.

Had that been unnecessary? He'd been out for months and hadn't looked for her at all? More bizarre, he'd become religious? The guy who'd cheated on his fiancée with more than one woman? None of it added up.

More, though, the few times she'd checked in with her attorney about him, she'd told her he was still in jail. Why hadn't she mentioned that he'd gotten out, gone to the seminary?

Then again, her lawyer's life didn't revolve around what Joshua did. Charlie's had, though.

Had all her caution been for nothing? She couldn't decide if she was more relieved or angry about that. She'd given up her spontaneity. For what?

As she tucked her armful of paperwork into her bag, she hurried for her car, watching over her shoulder.

She wondered if she'd always be looking behind her from now on.

* * * *

"Zip-lining, huh?" When Charlie had called him earlier and asked him to meet her at the zip-lining place in Mount Hood National Forest, Hunter had asked if he misheard her. She'd only laughed and repeated the address.

As if he didn't know where it was.

She adjusted the harness, making certain the carabiners were where the instructor had told them to put them. She grinned up at him. "Well, you can't introduce me to bungee-jumping and parachuting and think that would be enough for me."

He laughed. Never would he have guessed that he'd be creating an adrenaline junkie when he asked her to bungee with him the first time. "Watch out or you'll be skydiving soon."

Her brows dropped. "Isn't that the same as parachuting?"

"No. In skydiving, there's more freefall."

She considered for a moment. "You do that, too?"

"That might be my limit." After his drop last year, he'd had enough free-falling to last a lifetime.

"Huh. Interesting." She went back to her ties and buckles.

"Please tell me you aren't considering it." When she didn't immediately answer, he couldn't conceal his shock. "Charlie?"

She grinned up at him, and he chuckled, shaking his head.

God it was good to be here, with her. For the first time this week, he'd been able to relax. Training was winding down, but he spent more time second-guessing whether smokejumping was the right fit for him.

There was a lot of waiting around, he heard. On some level, he'd known that was the case. His father, his brother... It wasn't as if he wasn't familiar with the job requirements. But he hadn't faced how he would react to the job's spurts of extreme intensity amidst all the downtime. He'd been bored sometimes with the hotshots, but not like this. As a kid, he'd been unable to sit still. How was he going to manage days-long stretches of waiting?

He breathed out, running a hand over his face. This wasn't the time to worry. He hadn't seen his girl all week, and now was the time to enjoy her company.

Finishing his buckles, he followed her to the tower.

They were going to zip from one side of the mountain across the ravine to the other side. It was the perfect weather—clear, bright—and the spring had made everything green. As he climbed the stairs to the platform, he allowed the sounds of the forest to wash over him and the crispness of the air to ease the knot in his chest. Being in the open always made things better, especially when it was paired with the opportunity to do something that got his heart racing.

Like spending time with Charlie. And zip-lining wasn't so bad either.

There was another group on the platform when they got there, so they stepped to the back. A woman his mom's age had all her gear on but was wavering, eyeing the drop from the platform skeptically.

"Don't get me wrong, Char, I love this stuff. But why not picnicking or hiking?" He crossed his arms over his chest, looking her over. "Hard to catch up on the week riding a zip line."

The wind was playing with her hair, tossing the curls around her face. It might be sunny, but it was still cool out, lifting a flush on her cheeks. She'd grown up everywhere, but the mountains of Oregon complemented her.

She caught her bottom lip between her teeth. "Joshua is in a seminary."

"I'm sorry, what?" Maybe the wind had caught the words, because he wasn't following the conversation.

"I found out that Joshua isn't behind any of the stuff happening. Not the woman with the gun and not the break-in. He's studying to become a monk or something." She waved her hand, as if she were swatting away an insect. From what she'd told him of her ex-boyfriend, there were similarities.

"Are they certain it isn't him?"

"Apparently he's not allowed to leave. He's become quite devout, they said." She blew a raspberry, telling him how she felt about that. "So it's not him."

As the older woman finally decided to latch on and zip-line, he searched for an appropriate response. He doubted she needed the frustration racing through him. He figured she had enough of her own. Because if it wasn't Joshua the Dick, then who the hell was it?

Voicing that question wouldn't be helpful either. His worry for her was probably nothing compared to her own fears.

All he could ask was, "How are you doing?"

She snorted. "What can I do?"

The helplessness in her question struck a nerve in him. He'd been there, hadn't he? Sometimes, there were things out of your control. Times when the only option was to keep going. He understood that all too well.

She sighed, stepping closer and looking up at him. Where there had been derision a moment ago, now there was vulnerability. He wrapped his arms around her, drawing her closer, trying to be the strength she needed. "I decided, then, if there's nothing I can do about that, that doesn't mean I stop living. And this?" She motioned to the zip line. "This makes me feel alive. Jumping off bridges and out of airplanes with you has reminded me that I have to live right now, not worry about what might happen."

He held her against him, tucking her head under his chin. It was good advice—living in the moment. He had spent so much of the past year trying to get back to training. He'd been angry that his accident had derailed him, bitter at his brother for causing it, even unintentionally. All that working for the future, thinking about the next thing he needed to do, didn't leave him much time to spend in the present.

Maybe that's what he was doing with his training. Getting back to the RAC and becoming a smokejumper had felt like a finish line. Now he was there and it felt like he had so much left to do, as if his carrot had been moved. He was still working hard to accomplish his goal. Maybe he'd been too busy focusing on getting where he was, he'd forgotten that the whole process was a journey, that there wasn't an end point to reach. He'd always want to get somewhere else, to do something new, to push the next boundary.

Wasn't that what Charlie was doing, pushing forward? Maybe he needed to take her lead.

"You're right. Sometimes there is nothing to do." He held her at arm's length. "But we have now. Let's ride down this line."

Her face split into a bright smile. "Yes."

They stepped up, allowing the spotter at the top to recheck their gear. Neither of them hesitated when it came time to let go and leave the platform. Charlie might have jumped.

As he rode through the air, the carabiner scraping against the line was the only sound. He allowed himself to stay there, hanging over the open space. He didn't think about his accident, what it felt like to fall. He didn't think about his upcoming graduation and job at the RAC. Instead, he watched Charlie, with her curls blowing around her face, as she went in front of him, and he smiled.

That moment was pretty perfect. They'd take whatever was coming a step at a time.

Chapter Fifteen

With hardly any fanfare, Hunter's smokejumper training ended.

His mom threw a barbecue at her place, her pride evident. And, if he wasn't mistaken, there was some relief. He didn't want to dwell on that, or how much she'd probably worried for him this past year.

His friends came, guys from the hotshots, some of the other new jumpers. Meg and Lance were there; even Mitch showed up. There were sandwiches, burgers, salads, and beer. Charlie curled next to him, her smile a testament to how happy she was for him.

He suspected that most of them were proud that he'd finished. Just over a year ago, he'd been bedridden, his leg and arm broken. Worse, his brother was in custody and his uncle had killed himself. Back then, they'd questioned whether he'd ever be able to walk again, let alone finish training.

For them, this was a joyous occasion, representing his perseverance.

Except for Hunter, it was supremely anticlimactic.

He wasn't sure what he had expected to happen, but a firm handshake from Mitch and some other Forest Services brass wasn't exactly it. Even the camaraderie of the other smokejumpers didn't relieve the ache that he was missing something. He didn't know what it was, though, so he smiled and accepted everyone's pats on the back and pretended he was thrilled that he'd accomplished the milestone.

Not that he wasn't proud. He was. He'd worked hard, and it was a huge achievement. No denying that. This was everything he'd set out to do. As a smokejumper, he was the top of the firefighting food chain. The summer would be busy, and he would follow in his family's footsteps, fighting wildfires through the West. It was a life to be proud of.

His grin tightened as he made small talk.

When most of the guests were gone and only his family, Lance, and Charlie remained, his mother shooed him away. "Go home." She waved a towel at him, a trash bag in the other hand. Scooping a few empty plates in, she said, "You look exhausted. You can come help me clean up tomorrow."

"Stop," he said, throwing some empties into a recycling bin. "You know Meg'll have this place sparkling in a few hours."

His sister peeked her head around the corner. "I heard that." She shook the Windex container at him.

He rolled his eyes, waving at her. "See? Point, made."

"Seriously." His mother lowered the bag, leveling him with a more serious stare. "You look exhausted."

"Gee, thanks, Mom." No one could check a man's ego better than his mother.

Charlie sidled up beside him, tucking her arm under his. "I've got him, Mrs. Buchanan. I'll make sure he gets home safe." Like always, her body curved into his, as if it were meant to fit there.

His mother smiled at Charlie. "Thank you, Charlie, dear." As soon as Charlie turned back to straighten some cushions, his mom mouthed, "I like her," before scraping a bunch of napkins into the trash.

He grinned back, because it had been amazing to watch his mom fall for Charlie. He'd introduced them earlier that day, and they'd hit it off.

It wasn't hard to like Charlie.

"We can't leave." He glanced at the mess. "We should help."

"Hunt," Lance called from the kitchen, his sleeves rolled up and his hands soapy. "Go. We got this. It was a party for you. You don't clean up."

"Listen, you aren't trying out for favorite son around here, pal. I have that wrapped up," Hunter called to his friend.

In response, his mother chuckled, pulling him in for a hug. Then, low enough for only him to hear, she said, "I'm so proud of you, baby." When she retreated, her eyes were full and the moment tightened with emotion. "Your father would have been proud, too."

Hunter's throat thickened. She was right. This was his father's dream, that his sons follow in his footsteps, protect the land, protect its families. That, at least, gave him comfort in what was otherwise a confusing completion of training.

So much had happened this past year. His brother's incarceration and continued estrangement, his uncle's suicide, and his accident and subsequent rehabilitation. But while that had all been horrible, there were good things, too. Meg and Lance's impending marriage. His mother had grown stronger and closer to all of them, becoming more like the mother he remembered from his childhood every day.

And he'd met Charlie. As he tucked his mother against him, his gaze caught hers. She'd caught her lip between her teeth, obviously trying to hold her own tears in.

Tonight, she'd been quiet. She'd stuck close to his side, obviously happy for him, but she hadn't been her usual, vivacious self. They hadn't spent much time together this week. It was his last week of training, and she'd been busy with clients in Bend. Besides the trip to zip-line, they'd talked on the phone a few times, but it had been short, usually because he'd been exhausted.

As they walked outside to the driveway, she wrapped her arm around his. "You okay to drive?"

He'd barely gotten to finish two beers the whole night, thanks to everyone stopping to congratulate him. "Yeah. I'm fine." He kissed her on the top of the head, and she sighed.

In the car, she squeezed his hand and said, "So, you want to tell me what's going on in your head?"

He turned the key in the ignition, his brow furrowing. "What do you mean?"

"You might be able to pull that off with your family, but I've been watching you. Something's wrong. What's going on?"

He started the short drive to his duplex from his mom's place. How much should he tell her? He'd mentioned before that training wasn't what he'd expected, but did it matter? He'd already signed on to jump this year, and he wasn't the sort to back out of a commitment.

His jaw clenched. Was that what he was doing, considering quitting? After everything he'd been through to get here? He'd put in the work. This had been his dream for years, since he was a child.

He'd nearly died getting to this spot. He couldn't give that up now.

So what was his problem?

"It still feels off, that's all," he finally answered. "I thought it would be better, after training. But now that I'm here, it doesn't." That was as diplomatic as he could manage.

She didn't say anything for a long moment, and then she squeezed his fingers. "Maybe it doesn't feel right because it wasn't what you expected. Whether you expected it to be better or worse, maybe you're let down that it doesn't live up. Or, maybe you keep expecting it to get worse." She shrugged. "After all, the last time you were on this path, it didn't end well. Maybe you're preparing yourself for that."

Could that be all this was? Sure, he'd imagined what it would be like to be a smokejumper a million times, even more since being derailed last year. He'd wrestled with jealousy, with worries that he'd never be ready. Maybe it was that the reality was a letdown.

But as he cast a glance at her, that wasn't what nagged at him. It was that she wasn't only talking about him.

He pulled into a parking spot in front of his place, shifting the car into park before he turned to her. As he gathered her hand in his, he asked, "Is that what you're doing, Charlie? Preparing for the worst?"

"What do you mean?" She looked away, away from his eyes.

"I know I've been busy this week, finishing training, but things have been off. Is that what's going on?"

Her mouth thinned, and he wondered if she'd lie, tell him that everything was fine. That she'd only been having a hard week. Finally, though, she sighed.

"I thought it was him. I expected it to be him. Now, not knowing who it is…" She shook her head. "It's way worse. I keep waiting for the other shoe to drop. I haven't been able to move forward with Leslie to buy into the practice…I'm having trouble sleeping. I want to live in the moment, but I can't because I can't shake the feeling that someone is out there, wanting to hurt me."

He'd been busy this week. He should have gone to Bend to see her more, check on her. He'd texted and called, but that didn't make up for hands-on check-ins. After the break-in last week, she probably could have used some company.

"Maybe it's a coincidence." He rubbed circles into the back of her hand. "The addict? She was clearly far gone. And the burglary? It could have been anyone. You live downtown. Who knows what riffraff might have wandered in."

"And the advertisement?" she asked quietly. "What's your explanation for that?"

He didn't have an explanation for that. She must have read that on his face, because she shook her head.

"Come on, Hunter." She nudged her head toward the door. "Let's go in. It's supposed to be a celebratory night, not a night for us to be worrying."

His first instinct was to pressure her. The way she was processing all of this didn't feel right. But she had been trying so hard to focus on the present, to not worry about the future right now. He wanted to give her what she wanted.

He nodded and got out, walking around to grasp her hand as she stepped up on the sidewalk. As he opened the door and ushered her in, he barely had a chance to close it before she tumbled into his arms. She reached for him, dragging his mouth down to hers, and he obliged, kissing her with every bit of the emotion rushing through him.

Her kiss said that tonight, she didn't want to think about who might be trying to scare her.

He aimed to drive the foreboding away.

Reaching under her, he hiked her up, wrapping her legs around him. Still kissing, he carried her into the living room. He lowered her gently onto the couch, following her down. But she wasn't still, yanking at her shirt and pulling it over her head, then unsnapping her bra, all the while leaning up and into him. He tried to slow her down, but she was reaching for him. Then her breasts pressed against his chest, and everything went into overdrive in his brain.

They tore off the rest of their clothes, the frantic pace mirrored in the racing of his heart. As she coaxed him forward, he barely remembered the condom in his pants pocket. He leaned down, his limbs twisted with hers, to get it.

It was the fastest condom application he'd ever managed.

Then he was inside her, and they both let out exhalations that were part groan and part sigh. He closed his eyes, pausing to be present and there, as close to this woman he cared about as he could be.

But she wasn't having any of it. Shifting beneath him, she pulled away and then strained against him. His fingers flexed into the cushions next to her head, where he was holding himself up, and he moaned under the friction of it.

There was no slowing them now. She edged him forward, and her pace hitched up his own desire. Sweating as he approached the edge, he reached between them, rubbing the spot where they were connected. She cried out as she squeezed him tightly, sending him over the edge with her.

They lay in the silence afterward, panting and holding each other.

She had used this to distract herself from whatever fears and concerns remained. He understood that, and he didn't mind.

He had no problem being her shelter tonight.

Gathering her against him, he lifted her up and walked with her cradled in his arms toward his bedroom. After he deposited her on the bed, he went to the bathroom and made quick work of cleanup and condom disposal. Then he returned to her side, crawling under the covers with her and dragging her close, tucking the comforter around them.

Tomorrow, he would suggest that they meet with the investigator again. He'd talk to Dak and Heidi. Heidi was a Forest Services investigator. She might be able to come up with avenues they could explore, things they hadn't come up with on their own.

And he'd keep a closer eye on Charlie. He should have guessed this would tear at her and known that she wouldn't tell him about it. From here on, he'd pay attention.

It'd be his job to make sure she didn't hide inside herself.

* * * *

Charlie slept in at Hunter's. That meant she got a late start getting home, which got her a later start heading into the office to do some paperwork on Sunday afternoon.

Since she'd taken off some time to work with the investigators, she was behind. She figured she'd go in and get caught up before Monday's clients.

She stopped for coffee at the local place, getting some salted caramel something or another because the girl recommended it. Sipping, she could see why it was a favorite. Sweet and caffeinating, her favorite kind of beverage.

She sighed, happy at the normality.

In the spring sunshine, she allowed herself to breathe in and enjoy a beautiful morning.

As she strolled toward her office, her latte in hand, she decided Hunter could be right. All of her scary experiences from over the past weeks could be an unfortunate coincidence. The addict on the street and the break-in might have had nothing to do with one another. And the advertisement? If someone had sent it from here, it might be a disgruntled client. Or even a helpful client who believed she should get a gun to protect herself.

That was creepy, but not as scary as one person being behind all of that.

Either way, Hunter was right that she shouldn't be drawing any conclusions without evidence.

Trying to juggle her drink and search for her keys, she propped her bag on her knee and fished through it.

The pops distracted her. Why was someone setting off fireworks in the middle of the afternoon? But then someone screamed and there was yelling. She ducked, covering her head. Was something falling?

Then she heard it: "He's got a gun."

She crouched down, her pulse picking up. There was a planter nearby, one of those huge concrete ones that people put trees in. She tucked herself behind it, trying to be as small as possible.

Around her, people were running. She peeked out at the street but couldn't see anyone.

A few more pops sounded, and she reached a shaking hand into her purse, the contents spilling onto the pavement next to her and her spilled drink. She tucked her body further between the building and the planter, her fingers fumbling as she attempted to dial 911.

Another explosion and some of the concrete next to her sprayed, hitting her face and making her flinch. Then another spray.

The bullets were striking next to her. Through the numbness, all she could hear was the pounding of her heartbeat as shards of cement stung her skin. Around her, everything was moving. There were people running everywhere, ducking, and she could see their mouths moving. They were falling, stumbling, and dropping their personal items. But the sound didn't permeate the pulsing silence in her mind.

Her gaze wandered, falling on the phone in her hand. Her 911 dial had connected. She lifted the phone to her ear. Without waiting for any response on the other line, she said, "Hello? Someone is shooting at me."

She had to ask the operator to repeat their questions, but when she could finally focus, she hastily relayed the information. Sticking her finger in her other ear in a futile attempt to drown out the gunshots, she attempted to remain coherent. When sirens sounded, the pops stopped.

She had no idea how long she sat there, behind that planter, breathing. When she glanced at the phone still in her hands, she realized the call to 911 was still connected. That shouldn't confuse her. Vaguely, she remembered that they weren't supposed to hang up.

"Ma'am?" The voice startled her and she cried out. A policeman crouched on the sidewalk next to her, reaching for her. "Are you Charlie Jones? You called 911."

She had to clear her throat before any sound would come out. "Yes. I'm Charlie Jones."

"You can come out now, ma'am. The gunman is gone."

"Gone? As in, dead?" Had someone been killed while she huddled behind a bush?

He shook his head. "No, ma'am. Took off. Officers in pursuit. But you're okay now."

She doubted that, but she allowed him to help her to her feet. She patted her clothes, desperate to get the concrete dust that covered her off. On the ground, everything from her purse littered the sidewalk. Her makeup, her wallet. Seeing her personal belongings scattered around seemed like an invasion of privacy. She stooped, sweeping her things back into her bag. Except her fingers didn't work. They tingled, pins and needles like they were asleep. That's when she noticed her cheeks were damp. She swiped at them, coming away with moisture.

Was she crying?

The police officer didn't seem to know what to do, so he crouched, dragging everything he could find and depositing it into her bag. Together, they cleaned up the remaining items. Then he led her to his cruiser wordlessly.

She followed, her arms wrapped around herself.

As he filled one of his fellow officers in, she stood, watching the chaotic scene. There were other policemen asking witnesses questions, and they were all pointing and shaking their heads. Every face seemed to say the same thing: *I don't know what happened.*

She couldn't say that, though, could she? She was willing to bet that when they pooled all of the gunshot sites, they'd find most of them had been centered around her. A bunch of them had hit close enough to spray her with debris. Pretending anything else would take more denial than she could work up.

As she sat in the open car door of the cruiser, waiting for them to interview her, she stared at the sign for her therapy office. A week or so ago, she had been considering buying into it, setting up roots here, in Bend. Had it only been a handful of days?

Now, as she studied it, she couldn't imagine ever feeling safe here again.

Would they catch the shooter? Even if they did, would he be able to give them any indication of what was going on or would she be stuck wondering again, having no clue why she was being targeted?

The possibility made her stomach clench.

She couldn't live like this. She'd been threatened with weapons, shot at, and her home had been burglarized. What if someone she cared about had been with her today? Leslie, Meg, or even Hunter? The gunman had missed her, but there wouldn't have been enough room behind the planter for two people to hide.

If Hunter had been with her, he'd have tried to shield her. Where she'd been nauseous before, now her body was icy.

She wouldn't have been able to live with herself if something had happened to him. Even if she could manage the risks she was taking for herself, she wouldn't tolerate putting her loved ones in jeopardy.

As the police officer joined her, she asked, "Did they catch him?"

His mouth thinned. "They're still looking."

Which meant no.

Her chagrin must have been on her face, because the officer took out a notebook, and determination wrinkled his brow. "Don't worry, ma'am. We'll get him." He nodded, as if convinced of his colleagues' competence.

Right now, Charlie wasn't feeling as certain.

"What can you tell me about this?" he asked, his pen poised.

She launched into all of the things that had happened to her, explained how she suspected that she was the target. When his eyes widened, he folded his notepad and said, "Maybe you should come with me to the department. So we can piece this into your file."

It was overwhelming. She got that. She nodded, swinging her feet into the cruiser. As she rode the short distance to the police department with him, though, she couldn't shake the feeling that they were missing pieces of the puzzle.

And by the time they found them, it'd be too late.

Chapter Sixteen

After receiving Charlie's voicemail, Hunter arrived at her apartment in record time.

When she opened the door after he rang the bell, he folded her into his arms, breathing in the curls on her head. His eyes closed, and he allowed the strands of panic that had been attempting to weave their way through him to dissipate.

She tucked her head against him, dropping her forehead to his chest. He wasn't sure if he expected her to cry, but she only gripped his shirt tightly.

When he finally found his voice, he asked, "Did they find him?"

The rub of her forehead against him was a headshake, not a nod. "No. He took off as soon as the police showed up."

Damn it. Another dead end. He still couldn't believe that someone had tried to shoot her. The holdup, the break-in...but an actual attempted murder?

Again, he tamped down on the rage slicing through him. Someone had tried to kill her. It was unforgivable.

"Do the police have any idea what is going on here?"

She pulled away, and he immediately missed her body's warmth. Add the new distance on her face, and he wanted to sweep her up again and never let her go. "They have no idea what's going on."

"They're going to figure it out, Charlie. You haven't been here that long. You don't know that many people. They'll be able to find the link, I'm sure of it." He didn't have the words to convince her that everything would be okay.

"I'm glad you are, because I'm definitely not." She sank down on the bed in her room.

Only then did he see the suitcase. Her face was closed, as if an argument had been fought—and lost. "What's going on?"

"I called my parents. I haven't spoken to them in a while, but I tracked them down and I'm going to visit with them." She lifted her phone off her bed, checked it, and threw it back down. "I explained what was going on, and they're worried."

"Wait, you hadn't told them?" He couldn't imagine a world in which his mom didn't know that he'd been shot at. "Why not?"

"You don't understand my parents." She waved him off. "They were busy. I didn't want to bother them."

She was right. He didn't understand her parents. How could being kept up-to-date about their daughter's well-being be a bother? "You make it sound like you're an inconvenience."

She blinked at him, but she didn't rebuke his assumption. "It shouldn't be any problem for me to stay with them for a little while. It will give the police time to do their jobs."

"You're leaving?" The panic he thought he'd left in the car sprang forward again, full force.

"Not forever." She offered him a smile. "Just for a week or so." But her movements were jerky, as if even they knew she was lying.

"Charlie, no." Reaching her in a long stride, he gathered her hands in his. "Come on. Give the police a little time. These kinds of investigations are difficult. Did they tell you that they could do anything else to keep you safe?"

"They offered to do additional patrols of my house. But they couldn't give me round-the-clock protection. Because they don't know what they're protecting me from." Her mouth tightened, and he could see her frustration. She exhaled shakily and attempted a smile. As if it was fine that she needed protection from an unnamed threat.

But the smile did nothing to conceal her fear. She'd already been in danger before, in Chicago. Living under that kind of constant threat was exhausting. Doing it twice in a lifetime... Well, he could see why she was ready to run.

"Stay with me, then." He was probably holding her fingers too tightly, but he got the impression that if he let go, she might disappear.

She lifted her gaze to his, her eyes pleading, but her voice remained even, as if she were trying to pacify him. "What then, Hunter? Whatever horrible thing chasing me finds you, too?" Her grip tightened. "You know what I thought today, after they pulled me out from behind the concrete planter where I was hiding? As I brushed the debris from the gun blasts off of me, I couldn't stop thinking that there wasn't enough room back there for two people. What if someone I knew, someone I cared about, had been with me while I was the target of that gunman? What if someone I cared about—someone I loved—had been shot because of me?" Her eyes were full of pain, and she whispered, "I couldn't live with that. Please, don't ask me to."

Oh God, she'd been hiding behind a planter? He closed his eyes, hiding the flare of anger that came over him.

He wiped her hair out of her eyes, cupping her cheeks in his hands. Then he dropped kisses on her upturned face, desperate to wipe the uncertainty and panic away. She closed her eyes, gripping his forearms, her breathing shallow.

But he couldn't kiss this away. He had dealt with guilt, had worried about what could have happened. That was heavy weight to bear.

His brother had caused his accident. Not directly, but it was close enough. Will had twisted the parachute he'd worn, believing Lance would get it. He'd expected to scare the other man, to get him to quit rookie training. If Will was to be believed, he hadn't meant to hurt anyone. He'd expected Lance to cut his first chute and deploy his reserve.

But when Hunter had gotten the twisted parachute, he'd panicked. When he'd gone for his knife, it had slipped in his sweaty palm, and he'd been left with a jammed parachute. He'd attempted to detach it, but he'd been racing for the ground, running out of time. Lance had saved him, but he hadn't recovered well, landing hard.

There were so many things about that jump that could have gone differently, things that could have left others hurt—even killed—instead. While his own recovery had been long and arduous, he wouldn't have wished any of what he had dealt with on anyone else.

"What are you going to do, then, Char? You going to run away?" he whispered, still holding her face.

She didn't open her eyes but shook her head, her face rubbing against his hands. "I'm not running. It's a trip. To let the police do their jobs."

She stepped back, breaking the contact and returning to the clothes on the bed, stacked in neat piles. Folding, she still didn't make eye contact. "I'll stay for a week, maybe two. The police have all of my information. They can keep going without having to worry about protecting me or any of the people around me who could get hurt, too."

The way she mapped it all out sounded like she was convincing herself. It didn't tell him anything about what was going on in her head.

"Then why do I feel like I'll never see you again?" His voice broke. Apparently he couldn't hide any weakness from her. He should have known. She'd been there for his panic attacks and doubts about his future. Why pretend with her?

Her hands stilled on her clothes, and her head dropped. So he was right. She was running. He wanted to be angry, but he could only manage a bittersweet sympathy. Of course she was afraid. Who wouldn't be?

"Are you ever planning to come home?" He wanted to ask if she planned to return to him, but the words lodged in his throat.

Sinking down on the bed, she gazed up at him. "Hunter, I don't know what's going to happen. You have to understand how hard all of this is."

"I do understand. Truly. But instead of staying here, standing your ground, you're giving up." He shook his head. "You've been running your whole life. Don't you want to stop?" He wanted her to stop, to stay with him. To lean on him when she was afraid.

Color burst onto her cheeks, and she stood. "I have not been running. You don't really know me that well."

"Oh, I know you, Charlie Jones." He reached for her hand, but she remained out of his reach. "When we met, I feel like we recognized each other. When you're around, I can sense you, as if we're tied together, linked somehow. You can't pretend you don't feel that."

When her head dropped again, he reached for her, gripping her shoulders. "If you do, then stay. Fight for this." *Fight for us,* he meant.

But when she looked up again, she was already gone. "Some of us aren't like you. You"—she waved his hand over him—"you kept going, even after the worst happened. I'm not that person. I'm not that strong. And I won't put you or anyone else I care about in danger." She inhaled, but he could hear how much she struggled to remain in control. "Some of us aren't made for staying when things feel lost. I'm sorry."

The statement covered so many things. That he stayed after nearly dying in smokejumper training last year, obviously. But his heart said she was trying to warn him that she wouldn't stay when things got hard with them, the same as she didn't plan to stay now.

He retreated, tucking his hands in his pockets to keep from reaching for her. If he thought it would help, to hold her, even to make love to her, then he'd do it. If he thought touching her would change her mind, he'd never take his hands away from her.

But she didn't need him to hold her. She needed to see this differently than she did. And he didn't know how to make that happen.

"I'm sorry, too. Because I'm the kind of guy who does stick it out. And I'd stick around with you, if you gave it a chance, too."

He waited, holding her gaze. She looked away first.

The silence elongated, filling the space between them. His heart ached and, the persistent panic threatened to block his throat. He swallowed hard, trying to tamp it down. He'd relied on her, this connection between them, to soothe himself. That wasn't fair, not to either of them. He needed to stand on his own now.

"All right, then. I wish you the best." He backed out of the room, rubbing his palms on his thighs and trying to hold it together. "Let us all know when you're there, okay?"

She nodded, her throat working. He couldn't watch her let him go. Spinning, he left.

* * * *

Charlie dragged her suitcase out to her car, letting it thump down the few steps out front.

Hunter had left a few hours ago, and she was still second-guessing whether she'd done the right thing.

He didn't understand. She was running away? No, she was giving the police time to do their job without her there to be a distraction. She was a phone call away if they had any questions.

He'd basically called her a coward. Not in as many words, but it had been pretty damn close. She loved him, but maybe she'd read him wrong.

It sure wouldn't be the first time.

She clicked the key fob to open her car door. Wrestling the huge suitcase down the sidewalk, she left it on the curb as she lifted the hatch on her car. Swinging the luggage off the step, she was grateful for every workout she'd done recently. That thing was heavy.

She'd been too preoccupied with her mammoth luggage to see the woman standing next to her car. It wasn't until she straightened that she noticed the knife. A moment later, it was buried in her side.

Pain sliced through her and she cried out, stumbling back, her hand pressing to the wound. When she pulled her fingers away, they were sticky with blood.

The woman with the knife was staring at it as if she wasn't sure how it had gotten in her hand. Her pause gave Charlie time to reach into her pocket and pull out the pepper spray she'd bought today on her way home.

How she had the brain function to unlock it and point it properly, she might never guess. But when she sprayed it, her attacker fell to the ground writhing and screaming in pain.

Some other time, under other circumstances, she might have experienced sympathy for the girl, but right now, with blood gushing from her side, she couldn't work up much of anything.

Tripping, she hurried inside, her hand pressing more firmly over her wound. Though initially the stab had felt more like a punch, now the pain radiated down her side, stealing her breath.

She fumbled in her purse for her phone, keeping an eye behind her for the woman she'd sprayed. As she picked it up, she dialed 911. When someone answered, she said, "Yes, I've been stabbed. The woman is still here."

She hurried to give her location as she shuffled down the stairs, still bleeding and in misery. But she needed to make sure the woman was still there, still down. That she was in control. When she reached her attacker, she saw the woman still writhing on the ground, obviously in agony.

It was irrational, but Charlie wanted to spray her again. According to the directions, though, people who had been sprayed would take between fifteen and forty-five minutes to recover. No way she was getting up anytime soon. But the pain stretching up Charlie's side wasn't making her charitable.

Dizzy and hurting, she lowered herself to the ground, trying to breathe through the agony. As she stared up at the sky and her moans melted into the woman's, she wondered what Hunter was doing right that minute. Was he thinking he should have stayed, tried to talk her out of her decision?

Right now, bleeding on the sidewalk, cradling the pepper spray in case the woman became threatening again, she wished he would have stayed, too.

Chapter Seventeen

When Hunter stepped up to the nurses' station later that evening, he already expected to be turned away. Still, being asked what his relationship was to Charlie was a bit of a sore point.

He was nothing to her. He'd left her alone today.

He spun away, his helplessness so intense he choked on it. She'd been here—alone—for almost two hours. Meg had called to ask if he needed her to pick him up on the way. Confused, he'd needed to ask where they were going. Because Charlie hadn't reached out to him.

Burying his hands in his hair, he lifted his eyes to the ceiling. She could be dying in there. He wouldn't have had any idea.

The kind-eyed nurse smiled at him, telling him that it was only family right now to see her, and directed him to have a seat in the waiting room down the hall.

As he turned the corner, though, he found Lance and Meg. He stepped forward, folding his sister into a hug without a word. If he were a different guy, he might have argued that it was to support her. But he wasn't that guy. It was as much for him as it was for her.

Holding his sister helped him. It didn't stop the panic clawing at his stomach, but it took the edge off.

Pulling away, he asked, "What do we know?"

"Not much so far." Meg crossed her arms over her chest, her mouth tight. "She was brought in for a knife wound."

"Did she call you?" It was a small thing, but it stung that Charlie would call Meg and not him.

"No." Lance stepped forward, clasping him on the shoulder. "One of the guys on the hotshot crew is dating a cop. Recognized the name, met her at the engagement party. Knew she and Meg were friends."

It was a small world.

"A knife wound?" What the hell had happened? "Did they get the guy?"

"Woman." Meg nodded. "Charlie pepper-sprayed her."

"Since when did Charlie have pepper spray?" She would have told him that, wouldn't she? She'd never mentioned it. Then again, there were a lot of things he didn't know about her.

The way she'd let him go earlier? He never would have expected Charlie to be capable of something like that.

Meg shrugged. So Charlie hadn't told her either. That wasn't something she'd have left out. They were all worrying about her. She would have used the existence of a pepper spray to reassure them all, wouldn't she?

He had no idea. The past hours had made him question what he thought he knew about her.

A doctor finally came out, a face mask around his neck. "Meg? She's out of surgery."

She'd needed surgery? That revelation struck him in the gut. He remembered what going into surgery had felt like, when he was on oxygen and being rushed into the emergency room. The sounds and smells of the operating room rose in his mind, clobbering him with pain, hiking his pulse up until it roared in his ear. The noise was so loud that he almost missed his sister's question.

"Thanks, Carl. How did it go?" Meg folded her arms over her chest. Hunter forgot sometimes that Meg worked here, in Bend, as a physician assistant. Obviously she must know this guy. Bend wasn't a huge town.

"She came through splendidly. The knife missed all of the dangerous organs. She's got a fair amount of stitches and she'll be in a whole lot of pain, but she should make a full recovery."

Full recovery. That's what the doctor had said.

She would be okay.

He could breathe again.

The rest of the explanations were more detailed and better suited for his sister. All he'd needed was the reassurance that she'd be fine.

He faced the window, staring out, attempting to get his emotions in check. The scene was nothing to write home about—the top of the medical center. But it soothed him. He'd been in this hospital, last year. They'd taken good care of him.

His Charlie was in good hands.

Lance joined him, staring out at the lackluster skyline. "You okay?" he asked, under his breath.

Hunter could only nod.

"This is a good facility." Lance's voice was still low, private.

He jerked his head in agreement again. He'd forgotten Lance had spent time here, too, in the events surrounding his brother and uncle last year.

After another long moment, Lance said, "She's going to be okay."

"I know, man." Hunter's head dropped. "Thank God."

Lance patted him on the shoulder. Not a comforting pat, but the solid smack that said man-to-man that he believed in him. That he was sure Hunter had it together.

Biting his bottom lip, he desperately hoped his friend was right.

A couple of cops came from the same direction as the doctor. Hunter recognized one of them from his hotshot days. "Hey, Kendall."

The guy's mouth split into a grin. "Hey, man. How are you?"

"I'm okay. You here for Charlie Jones?" He tried to keep his tone light, but his concern was probably all over him.

Kendall was onto him, too. His eyes narrowed. "Yeah. You know her?"

"Yeah. We're close." He didn't know exactly what they were right now, but close definitely covered it. "They caught the attacker, right?"

"Yeah. Addict. Said she was paid to go after the girl. I didn't get much beyond that because she's tweaking and paranoid. But she said her dealer paid her." Kendall shrugged, lifting his hands.

"Her dealer paid her?" Hunter crossed his arms over his chest. "That's not how it usually goes, right?"

Kendall chuckled. "Definitely not."

"She give you the dealer's name?"

The cop shook his head. "Nothing beyond a street name. Runt. Probably some small-time kid. We'll follow it up. Meth, though. Stuff is messed up. If he's a smaller dealer, there's someone over him. We'll see what we can find out."

"Meth." The hairs on the back of his neck stood up. "Another meth addict raised a gun at her a month or so ago."

That was too much of a coincidence. There was no way Charlie had become a target of drug addicts by herself. Even if she'd been unfortunate enough to be in the wrong place at the wrong time twice, that they were both tweakers suggested something more organized.

Besides, this was Charlie. She drank smoothies with green stuff in them. She worked out religiously, was a physical therapist. She took her health seriously. There was no way she'd gotten tangled up with meth addicts on purpose.

But he had. And meth...

"Our only guess is that she did something to piss off someone in that food chain." Kendall's eyes narrowed. "Why? Do you have any ideas? Miss Jones was coming out of anesthesia when I last checked in on her. I wasn't going to bother her yet, give her a few hours. Is there something I'm missing?"

"Yeah. I think I know who you should be looking at." He put his hand on his stomach, suddenly ill. "Johnny Santillo. He might be targeting her to get back at me."

* * * *

When Charlie woke, Hunter was sitting next to her, holding her hand. The lazy circles he drew on the back of it calmed her, like all the other times he touched her.

Seeing him, she wondered if it was a mistake, if this was another hallucination from the anesthesia. She had some crazy dreams earlier, a bunch of stuff about bugs. As she stared at him, she realized she was itchy. Probably the painkillers. Any of the morphine derivatives would have made her itchy. They'd told her she was allergic when she had the same reaction the last time she'd needed them, after Joshua.

Probably explained the bug dreams, too.

Still, Hunter looked corporeal. She blinked a few times and he remained. Definitely real.

Except he shouldn't be here, should he? They'd had a fight. He'd told her she was running away.

Then she'd been stabbed.

Right now, his eyes were full of emotion, things she didn't understand. But she was obviously drugged, so maybe that was all in her head.

"Hey," he offered, breaking the silence. He dropped her hand onto the bed. As much as she didn't want to admit it, she missed the warmth of his touch.

"Hi." Her voice cracked, and the inside of her mouth felt like sandpaper. He must have noticed, because he retrieved the cup on the tray table next to them and lifted the straw to her mouth. She reached for it, only to be stopped by a sharp pull and a burn of pain on her side.

That's right. That's where she'd been stabbed.

"Take it easy," he said. "I got it."

She allowed him to hold the cup. Before she was done, he took it away, though.

"Not too much. So you don't get sick."

She nodded, shifting, but no position was comfortable. She didn't want to struggle in front of him, either. Giving up, she sighed, falling back onto the pillow. "What are you doing here, Hunter?"

He dropped his gaze, and she regretted the harshness. Trying again, she said, "Thank you for coming. I didn't expect you. That's all." She'd considered calling him. In fact, it was all she could think about as the ambulance drove her to the hospital. But the entire point of pushing him away had been to keep him safe. Asking him to be by her side now would be counterproductive.

"Yeah, well, I'm not sure you'll want to talk with me after what I'm going to tell you." He grimaced.

"What happened?" Excitement raced through her. "Did they find out anything from the girl who stabbed me?" She smiled at him. "I pepper-sprayed her."

"You definitely did." He offered her a half grin. "Great job."

Her triumph dimmed, though. "What do you mean after I talk to you?"

Seeing him here, his obvious concern, well, it was bad news. Not just because he was in danger here, with her, but it was risky for her heart. She loved him. She hadn't wanted to let him go, didn't want things to end this way.

Didn't want things to end at all.

Every second she spent with him weakened her resolve. Maybe, if they found out who was doing this to her, they could make it stop. She would be safe, especially now that Joshua had found the light or whatever. Things between them could return to the way they had been. She could buy into the therapy practice, and they could keep going as they'd been.

They could be happy.

When he didn't speak right away, her stomach sank further. "What's going on?"

"They did get some information out of the woman who stabbed you." He held her eyes, but his were full of apology. "She's an addict, meth. Like the woman who tried to shoot you last month."

"She is?" Two meth addicts. What did that mean?

"Yeah. I spoke with the police officer who questioned her." He toyed with the sheet. "He said the woman was paid by her dealer to attack you."

"Why would he pay her to attack me?" This was crazy. She wasn't connected to drugs, never touched the stuff. "I don't know any drug dealers or even people who do hard drugs. I smoked pot once in college, and I didn't like it. I'm not exactly the poster child for getting tangled up in drug wars."

"No. But I am."

"What?" What was he talking about? "You don't do drugs." She'd only gotten to know him well over the past couple of months, so she wasn't the expert of all things Hunter Buchanan. But she could say with reasonable certainty that he didn't use illicit substances. A man couldn't be as healthy and strong, accomplish so many physical milestones, without taking care of his body.

"No, but I helped put away a meth dealer a few years ago. Johnny Santillo. We stumbled on a couple of cooks in the forest, in an isolated lab set up in an RV. I helped them escape the cycle, get help. They ratted him out, put him in jail for all sorts of things, even human trafficking." He bit his lip, his jaw tightening. "Real piece of work. But, apparently he got out on good behavior recently. A couple of the guys at work were talking about it because there have been other explosions in the national forests, stuff the Forest Services has come across or been called in to manage. I didn't make the connection, not until this addict attacked you. One meth addict is one thing, two is a pattern when added to all the other things you've had to deal with."

It might have been because of the painkillers or leftover anesthesia, maybe exhaustion, but she wasn't sure she understood exactly what was going on. "You mean that this drug dealer—"

"Johnny Santillo," he supplied.

"Right. Johnny Santillo. You mean he's targeting me because of you?"

Hunter winced as he swallowed. "Yes. I think that's what I mean."

She could only blink at him. For weeks, she'd been worrying that her past relationship with Joshua was the reason she was suffering. That her old, bad judgment when it came to men was coming back to haunt her.

She hadn't considered that her current judgment was the root of her problems.

"Why?" That was the question echoing through her mind. "Why is he coming after me if he's angry with you?"

"I honestly have no idea." He shook his head, letting it fall low between his shoulders. "I don't know why he's doing this. If he has a problem with me, he should have taken it up with me, left you alone."

As she placed all of the incidents on her timeline, it became clear that she'd only started to run across trouble when she started spending time with him.

This creepy monster of a drug dealer had been watching her—or having his minions watch her—for weeks.

A sudden wave of nausea washed over her. "I think I might be sick."

With his signature quick reflexes, he pressed the nurse's call button and reached for the barf pan. She tried to turn to the side, to shield him, but she couldn't, not with the stitches. It didn't end up mattering, anyway. There wasn't anything in her stomach to throw up. Instead, she dry heaved in painful spasms.

As the reflex settled, her brain spun. What was she supposed to do with this information?

Hunter patted her back, rubbing her spine. "I'm so sorry. You have no idea how incredibly sorry I am for dragging you into this."

"You didn't do it." That was the real problem. He was as much a victim here, watching her suffer, as she was. "Where is this drug dealer, Santillo?"

He exhaled a heavy breath. "They don't know yet. But now that they have a direction to look for him, they can issue a search warrant, bring him in. Question people. Someone is going to want to flip on him. It's only a matter of time."

"What's going to happen to me, in that time?" She hated to sound selfish, but she was already hurt. "Now what?"

"They are going to increase your security. The cop I talked to said that they would put someone at your door here while you're in the hospital. And they'll reevaluate when you're discharged."

Except if this guy wanted to kill her, he had already proved he had henchmen at his beck and call, willing to go to whatever lengths necessary to accomplish the task.

"I really am sorry, Charlie." Hunter reached for her fingers again, squeezing them tightly. "I'm going to stay here, with you, as long as you want. I'll do everything I can to keep you safe. I've had some self-defense training. I'll watch over you while you're hurt."

Except then he would be in danger, too. What was the point of both of them being where this madman could find them? But if she told him that, he'd insist on staying. He would think of her first.

She wasn't about to let that happen. So while everything inside her wanted to scream for him to stay, she squeezed his hand and shook her head.

"I think I'd rather be alone for a little while, Hunter. This is a lot to take in. I know this wasn't anything you wanted, but I'd like a few days. To process." The words tasted gritty, and she had to swallow after they left her mouth. Because it was a lie. This wasn't his fault. But it was for his own safety. Otherwise, he wouldn't leave her side. She might not have known him long, but she knew he was that stubborn. Though all she wanted was to lean on him, to not be alone, she could never live with herself if something happened to him while he tried to protect her.

She'd leave, too, spend time with her parents until they could drag this Santillo guy in. Maybe when this was over she could explain. Apologize. But even as she hoped for the future, she wasn't sure he'd ever forgive her for this.

She wasn't sure she'd forgive herself.

He shifted back in his seat, pulling away from her. Her heart ached, right along with all of the other pains in her. She wanted to take it back, this distance she had put between them. But she refused to do that if it meant exposing him in additional danger.

She waited, saying nothing. She wasn't sure she could say anything right now anyway. The words were lodged in her throat, along with her heart.

Finally, he pushed his chair back, standing. He patted her hand. "I understand."

She had no idea what he understood. Nothing about this made any sense, especially how much she wanted to keep him next to her. Worse, she could only guess at the ways he was beating himself up right now, how much he must be hurting, too.

At the door, he paused, smiling at her. "Take care, okay?"

She nodded. If she spoke, she'd say something she'd regret.

Then he was gone, and she let the tears slip down her face.

Chapter Eighteen

"She's getting better, since you asked." Lance stepped behind Hunter's head to spot his bench press.

Hunter pushed the dumbbell up with more force than necessary before he answered. "I'm glad."

He wasn't sure he wanted to hear anything about how Charlie was doing. Well, he did. But hearing only made it harder. Meg was there, watching over her. So he was sure she was fine. Hearing about how fine she was, though...

No.

"You didn't ask." Lance spotted him through his last rep and then helped him set the bar on the stand.

He swung his legs over the bench, reaching for the towel to wipe off his brow. "Because I want to ask too damn much."

"That doesn't make a jack lick of sense."

"She said she needed space, Lance. She's in there because of me. I didn't stab her, but I might as well have. Put yourself in my position. If that was Meg in that hospital, would you want to give her space?"

"I don't think I would give her space. I'm kind of an asshole like that."

Hunter couldn't argue with that. Lance had never been known for his subtlety. "Meg's with her. There are policemen at her door. If she doesn't want to see my face, I can't say I blame her."

This morning, they'd picked up the dealer, Runt. Of course, he didn't know where his boss was, where he lived, anything. Because Johnny was a pro. He wasn't going to tell a two-bit dealer where he was. Dealers were caught constantly. The less they knew, the better for their bosses.

"That's a giant pile of shit. If you don't know that, you're a bigger idiot than I always thought you were." Lance crossed his arms over his chest. "And at times I've thought you were a huge idiot."

Hunter smirked at his friend. "Did I tell you her name isn't really Charlie Jones? It's Charlie Michaelson. She had to change it when she moved here to feel safe again after an old boyfriend beat her up."

Lance's usually easygoing expression fled and his face darkened. "What?"

"Yeah, some dickwad in Chicago. She pressed charges and he went to jail, though he's out now. Said he found Jesus or some shit, so now he's in some seminary or theological program or something." He snorted. "But what I'm saying is she's already been hurt by one guy she dated. And now here I am, screwing up her life."

"You didn't make Johnny Santillo target her, you moron. He did that on his own."

"I know. But she doesn't know him. I do."

Lance glared at him. But Hunter had been ignoring those glares for his entire life. When Lance spoke, his earlier frustration was gone. "This is your problem, man. You carry all this around all the time." Lance poked him in the chest. "In here. This guilt."

Hunter could only stare at him.

"You are wracked with it, and I don't understand it. But it's hurting you. And it's hurting her."

The words rang so clearly though him that Hunter had to look away. He was too raw right now to see the pain in his friend's face. Especially because he was right. There wasn't a morning over the past year that he hadn't looked in the mirror and put a mask on so he could keep his family and friends—the whole world—from seeing how much he was struggling. His mom and Meg? They worried about him too much already. His friends felt bad for him, and the rest of the world was watching him for any sign that he was breaking so they could drag him and his loved ones through hell again.

Because of him.

It had been hard, sure. It had been hard on all of them.

"The worst part," he whispered, "is that we can't find him anywhere. Santillo. He's nowhere, Lance." He slammed his palms on the bench next to him, shaking his head. "I have no way to keep her from getting hurt. I'm completely helpless."

That was what had kept him up last night. He hadn't put it together—that Santillo was behind it—until after she was injured. Even then, he had no idea how to track down Santillo. There were so many things that had already gone wrong.

So many things that could still go wrong.

He'd come so far, doing so much to put his life back together. But now, with Charlie in the hospital, it was as if he was back at the beginning, with everything out of his control.

The familiar tightness crept into his chest. But while often he could tamp down on the panic, today it rode through him. He couldn't breathe, and he gasped, staring wide-eyed at his friend.

This was it. He was going to die. His heart was going to give out. It couldn't race this fast without him having a heart attack, could it?

As he stood, pacing away from Lance, he pressed his palm against his chest, trying to calm his breathing, trying to focus on breaking the cycle.

"Hey, man. You okay?" Lance stood next to him, studying him. "What's going on?"

"Can't. Breathe," he gasped out.

"I'm getting a paramedic."

He stopped him, placing his hand on his arm. "No. Wait." Shaking his head, he held on to Lance's arm as the waves of panic washed over him. His friend humored him, standing next to him and shielding him from other eyes as he waited it out.

The long moments ticked by, and eventually Hunter's breathing returned to normal and he didn't vibrate with the beating of his heart.

"What the hell is going on?" Lance whispered, when Hunter finally got everything under control and sank down into a nearby chair.

"Panic attack." The words alone were damning. He hadn't said anything to anyone about the panic attacks. In the light of his friend's eyes, he could see that was a mistake. He hadn't been hiding them, though. Not really. He'd figured they'd go away, once he figured out whatever was causing them. He hadn't believed they were a big deal.

He hadn't wanted them to be a big deal.

Except they hadn't stopped. He had suspected they were caused by the jumps, the return to parachuting. But apparently not. He hadn't wanted to admit he didn't understand what was causing them.

"How long?" Lance asked.

"Months. Not often, but here and there." That was true enough. Most of the time, he could stop them, catch himself.

"You talk to anyone?"

Hunter shook his head.

Shouts rent the air as the signal for a fire went out. He stood. He was on the jump list. He was scheduled to go. As he headed for his equipment, Lance stopped him. "Listen. You need to talk to someone."

"Lance…"

"I'm serious. When we get back. You need to tell Mitch."

They held each other's gazes, and Hunter was reminded of stare-downs in elementary school. "Fine. When we get back."

Lance nodded, heading off to prepare for their jump.

Damn it. He didn't need to deal with this right now. Except he couldn't pretend that Lance wasn't onto something. He'd been ignoring the attacks, hoping they would go away.

Had he been in denial?

Shaking his head, he pushed the whole situation into the back of his mind. Lance was right. It was time he got to the bottom of it, when he got back. Right now, he was needed.

He trailed after Lance, hurrying to catch up.

* * * *

Meg sat in the chair next to Charlie's bed, her face a mixture of frustration and "are you crazy?"

Not that Charlie hadn't expected that response. She'd been wondering if she was crazy all day. When her friend sat down and demanded to know what she'd done to her brother, Charlie had confessed.

Now, she squirmed under Meg's glare.

"You let Hunter believe he was responsible for your injury so he would stay out of harm's way?" Meg's brow wrinkled, and she spoke slowly. As if the painkillers had impaired Charlie in some neurological way. "Do you know what that is going to do to him?"

"Yes. I mean, no. That's not exactly how it worked, Meg." She was making it sound worse than it was. "I was worried about him."

"I'm here, Char. You're not worried about my safety?"

"Of course I am." Charlie shifted, trying to get comfortable. Her stitches had started to ache today, but it wasn't time yet for another dose of painkillers. "But this drug dealer wants to get back at him, not you."

"I'm his sister."

"And you probably shouldn't be here either." The words were snappish, and Charlie sighed. "I'm sorry. I know you're worried about me."

"We all are." Meg reached out to hold her hand. "But while you'd rather push everyone away and run and hide when things get hard, that's not how I work."

Charlie stiffened. "I'm not pushing you away."

"You absolutely are. Pushing and then running. And it sounds like you have some practice."

"What? I told you that I left Chicago—"

"Oh, I get Chicago, hon. I do. If I'd needed to feel safe after something like that, I'd have left as well. No, I mean everything else."

Charlie glared at her. "I don't know what you mean."

"Your family moved around, didn't they? A lot."

"All the time. My parents liked trying out new places and experiences."

"So tell me about making friends. Did you have a lot of friends?"

"It's hard to make friends when you never stay in one place for longer than a year." She stiffened. She didn't want to relive how hard those times could be.

"I know you." Meg squeezed her hand, her eyes soft. "You don't have a hard time making friends. But you do have a hard time opening up to them."

That was so true that she couldn't even respond. Letting people in was not her forte. She had learned that if she got people to talk about themselves, she made friends more easily. Everyone liked to talk about themselves. And she was a good listener. Rarely, especially when she was a child or in high school, did her friends notice that she hardly said anything about herself.

At first, it was because she didn't want to talk about her weird family life. It wasn't strange to her, but she hated the questions people asked about her parents' nomadic lifestyle. About how they worked odd jobs and lived in hotels or short-term rentals. If it bothered her that her parents were often more concerned with what they wanted than whether she was making friends, she tried to keep that to herself.

She loved her parents. Watching her friends judge them had been difficult. So she stopped opening her life up for scrutiny.

Somewhere along the line it became a habit.

Meg's blue eyes didn't waver, appearing to see through her. Charlie squeezed her hand. "I never meant to hide anything from you. You're my closest friend." Her eyes stung. She hadn't meant to exclude Meg, to make it seem as if she didn't trust her with her past.

Maybe Meg was right. Maybe she'd been hiding.

"Can you hug me?" she asked, her voice small. "I would do it myself, but bending up might pull my stitches."

Her friend laughed, leaning forward and folding her in a gentle embrace, careful not to jostle her too much as the tension was broken.

"I'll do better," she whispered. "At least I'll try." As Meg pulled away, though, Charlie searched her face. "But I still think it would be smart to leave for a while. Give the cops a chance to find this guy. It'll be better for everyone if I'm not around. Especially Hunter."

"Does Hunter get a say in that?" Her friend's brows lifted. "You do know that if you aren't here, Santillo might go into hiding until you return, right? Not only that, but if you leave, you'll be looking over your shoulder for the rest of time. The cops know what's going on. Why don't you stay, keep your pepper spray close, and let them protect you? Let them do their job? And let the people who care about you watch out for you, too."

It was tempting to think about standing her ground, staring into the danger and saying that she wouldn't be pushed around anymore.

She'd always prided herself on living in the moment. She wanted this life, the life she was living right now. She wanted to stay in Oregon, buy into the physical therapy practice. She wanted to stay with her friends.

Stay with Hunter.

His face sprang to mind, and the pang at leaving him struck her hard in the stomach. Could she do that?

She loved him.

Wasn't that supposed to make her stronger, somehow?

"I'll think about it." She offered Meg a cautious smile. "I promise."

"That's all I can ask." Meg stood, squeezing her hand one more time. "But either way, you should come clean with Hunter. He's been through a lot already. He deserves the truth from you."

Unable to speak, Charlie swallowed and nodded as Meg left.

She wasn't sure if she agreed with everything else Meg had said, but that was the truth. Hunter had been amazing to her. She owed him an explanation, no matter what she decided.

* * * *

Hunter had been told that the first fire he jumped would be special. His colleagues were right.

As he got his tap on the shoulder, the sound of the plane's roar loud in his ear, he tossed himself out of the door and into the open sky.

The few moments before his parachute opened, free-falling toward the earth, his priorities reevaluated, crystallizing into the most important things.

He needed to talk with his sister, about his panic attacks, about how the last year of rehabilitation had deeply affected him. He'd hidden most of the difficult times from her, not wanting to tell her how hard things were. He could still remember the concern and pain that had been burned on his mother's and Meg's faces when he woke up after the accident. They'd been destroyed, worried, and he'd never wanted to see that kind of agony again.

As he'd gone through the painful process of recovery, he'd downplayed the difficulty. How many times he'd doubted that he'd ever be whole again. He'd hidden so much that his concerns had become secrets.

Meg would understand, though. She was a physician assistant. She would be able to guide him to someone who could help him figure out what was going on in his head.

He also needed to talk with Charlie. As the tug of his parachute opening and catching sent a rush through his stomach, her face flitted through his mind, another tug in his chest.

His suspicion that she was hiding something from him clarified. She had wanted him to walk away, had pushed him to do so. Why?

Well, she had said she needed time, but he wasn't the sort to give up. If she hadn't figured that out about him yet, then he would prove just how steadfast he could be.

When he got back from this jump, he'd fix things, with his head and with his heart.

As he floated to the ground, the plume of smoke from the fire he would be fighting trailed into the sky nearby, and for the first time in a long time he was at peace with his direction.

His landing went perfectly. Most important, he managed not to tree himself. In record time, he gathered his gear, stowed his jumpsuit, and headed off to meet the rest of his colleagues.

When they'd all huddled up around the crew boss, Tim, his face was grim. "It's a meth lab." He shook his head. "We're to assess the situation from a distance, but we're waiting on additional resources for hazmat containment."

Meth labs in the forest were becoming a much larger concern for the Forest Services. Because of the flammable materials involved, containing them could be tricky. The personnel working the fire had to be constantly aware of the chance for explosions or for exposure to potentially hazardous materials.

As they broke off and began the process of stopping the fire's spread and clearing a space for a helicopter to land with more specialized hazardous material personnel, he dug into the backbreaking work involved in this job. Smokejumpers might have the added difficulty of parachuting into the remote spaces that took longer for other firefighters to get to, but the methods of firefighting remained the same. Axes and debris removal, creating a barrier to keep the fire from reaching its fuel. The monotone of the physical labor and the science of burns.

He'd fallen into the motions, the natural high he got from repeated physical activity, so he didn't notice right away when the shouts from the rest of the team split the forest.

Two men were stumbling around, flailing. They might be in their teens, but he couldn't be sure. They were significantly aged, their faces pockmarked and their cheeks sunken. Probably the meth cooks.

And one of them was holding a gun.

Around him, the other jumpers had realized the same. They'd all attended the required training session on how pop-up meth labs were becoming a major issue for the government agencies involved in forest preservation. They were taught to stay away from anyone involved with the labs, as tweakers could be paranoid and erratic, disassociated from reality, so they were backing away slowly.

But, though the situation was dangerous, the coincidence was too much for Hunter.

It hadn't even been two days since Charlie had been stabbed, and now he was standing next to an explosive meth lab, facing two armed tweakers? The back of his neck tingled.

That wasn't a coincidence.

"Where's Buchanan?" The man with the gun yelled. "I'm looking for Buchanan."

The sickness in his stomach consolidated, even as his temper ignited. "Who's asking?"

"Santillo says that you're worth killing." The tweaker didn't look at anyone else, his attention directed at Hunter. He moved through the brush, his arm outstretched, the gun waving.

The other man stayed back, as if some part of his drug-addled mind recognized his partner wasn't getting him involved in anything good.

"You work for Santillo?" Hunter needed to keep him talking. If the guy remained focused on him, he wouldn't be looking at his friends.

"He says you ruined his life." The cook had to scream over the flames behind him.

"Think he probably did that himself," Hunter yelled back. Around him, the other jumpers were shifting back and away in an ever-expanding circle. To help shield them even further, he stepped forward, drawing the cook's attention.

The cook lowered the gun, putting it on the ground. "He's coming for you, you know. That's what he told me to tell you." He backed away from the gun. "He wanted me to tell you that after he kills your little whore, he's coming for you, too."

With that bit of prophetic rambling, he joined the other man and they sat down, their hands in front of them.

The crew boss had pulled his revolver, approaching the two cooks and keeping them in his sights. There was more shouting as someone else came forward with rope and the two men were subdued.

Lance approached him. "Hunter. You okay?"

He shook his head. This was so fucked that he wasn't sure he'd ever be okay again. "I need to get back to Charlie."

"Buchanan." The crew boss's revolver was holstered again, and he stalked toward them. "What the ever-loving hell is going on?"

"I'd like to go back with them. Have you radioed for a helicopter?"

"Christ." The boss ran his hand over his soot-covered hair. "Yeah. I did before, actually, when we found out it was a meth lab. Nothing has changed. We still need to clear a landing for it. That'll take some time."

"Understood. But when it's ready, may I go?"

"That's highly irregular." The boss glared at him. "Not sure if you noticed, Buchanan, but there's a fire over there. I need you."

"My girl." Hunter wasn't sure if he could call Charlie his girl any longer, but in his heart, that's what she was. He loved her. He wasn't sure that would change anything for her, especially with all of the trouble he'd brought into her life. But that didn't stop him from feeling that way. "She's in danger."

"We can call back, have someone check on her."

He nodded. "Please." He wanted to push, to demand to go. But what could he do there that the police couldn't do without him? He understood that he was better utilized here, fighting this fire.

Tim must have seen that on his face. "Damn it." He glanced toward the two cooks, now bound. "Fine. I'd want to go, too, if it was me. Let's go call back, explain what we can, call in law enforcement. But then you better work your ass off until they get here."

"Absolutely." As if there were any question.

Following the boss to the radio so he could relay information back to the base, Hunter couldn't help wondering, though, if the precautions they were going to take would be enough to keep her safe.

When he was finished, he hurried back to his Pulaski, digging in to clear the brush for the helicopter. The faster they finished this, the sooner he could lay eyes on Charlie.

Chapter Nineteen

Hunter boarded the helicopter with the meth cooks. He couldn't help himself; he attempted to get what he could out of them. The one who hadn't uttered a word since they'd found them in the woods kept silent. His eyes cast around frantically. Either he recognized how much trouble he was in or his paranoia was so high that everything around him looked dangerous.

The one who'd wielded the gun was more forthcoming, at least initially. He started with repeating what he'd said at the meth lab, that Santillo was coming for him. But when Hunter's line of questions turned to what—if anything—Santillo was going to do to help the cook, he clammed up, his eyes narrowing.

After calling to the air center so they could contact Charlie's guards and tell them what happened, Hunter spent the remainder of the trip back to Redmond berating himself. He was pissed and terrified, a horrible combination.

What if he didn't get to her in time? She could be in danger right now and he had been in the middle of a National Forest, leaving her to her own devices.

He should have seen it coming, but the panic attack hit hard, stealing his breath and filling him with doom. As his gaze bounced around the helicopter, he couldn't avoid comparing his own lack of focus with the two meth addicts next to him.

And even as the anxiety paralyzed him, he recognized that if he was with Charlie right now, he would be no help at all.

He'd spent all these months avoiding the reasons why he was having these episodes, pretending it wasn't an issue. He had done intricate mental gymnastics to convince himself that when some variable was removed from his life, they would go away. That variable had changed more than a couple times, until he had to admit that he had no idea what was causing the attacks. At first, he'd assumed they were linked to his first jump. After what had happened a year ago, it had been logical; facing another jump after that would be difficult.

He'd credited Charlie with his successful jump. He'd latched onto her as his strength, as a calming factor in his life. When he hadn't been able to talk to his family or his friends, he had been able to talk to her. He'd opened up to her in ways that had helped him, grounded him.

He'd believed she'd fixed him.

But was he broken? He had finished training, top of his class. By all accounts, he was physically recovered. He was dependable and worked hard.

He'd come so far, but he had to admit that he couldn't figure this out, and it bothered him that it remained out of his reach.

Why hadn't he asked for help earlier? When he'd talked with Lance at the base, Lance had been pissed. Hunter tried to put himself in Lance's position. If he'd watched one of his friends struggle, if he'd found out that Lance or Dak or one of his siblings had been struggling with panic attacks or anxiety and hadn't said something, he would have been upset. But mostly, he'd have been concerned, like Lance.

None of their accomplishments—personal or professional—would be worth his loved one's happiness. So why hadn't he treated his own health and happiness with the same regard?

He would have insisted they get help. Why hadn't he taken his own advice?

Except he'd been trying so hard to prove to them that everything was all right now. That even though last year's accident had happened, he'd recovered. He'd finished rehab, finished training, become a smokejumper like his family expected.

But maybe that was the problem. This wasn't about them. It was his life. He didn't need to prove anything to anyone but himself.

Lance was right. He'd let this get too far out of hand.

As soon as things settled down, as soon as Charlie was safe, he'd start the process. If that threatened his work at the air center, so be it.

This was his life. It wasn't perfect, but he wasn't broken either.

It was time he took back control. It was overdue.

When he arrived at the air center, he changed in record time before hurrying to his car. He dialed the hospital on his way, needing to hear what they'd done to ensure Charlie's safety. As he accelerated, his car eating up the miles between Redmond and Bend, he wouldn't relax until he saw her for himself.

* * * *

Charlie's eyes were heavy when the door to her hospital room opened after dinner, admitting a janitor cart. Two hours earlier, two detectives from the Bend PD had stopped by, explaining that Johnny Santillo had planted meth cooks in the forest to warn Hunter. They didn't know many details, but they were under strict orders to remain at her door and increase their vigilance.

She'd been unable to eat any dinner. She'd attempted a book but hadn't been able to concentrate, instead settling on reality TV.

Meth cooks had threatened Hunter. She'd processed that they had threatened her, too, but all she could focus on was that he'd been threatened.

Her whole point for being distant had been to try to keep him safe. Or so she'd told herself. Had she believed that would actually work?

She'd been protecting herself, not him.

She'd called Meg, who didn't have any additional information either except that Lance was on the jump with Hunter. Her worry had coursed over the line. When Meg had offered to come and sit with her, Charlie had declined. No reason for her to drive to Bend when Lance would be flying back into Redmond.

So instead, she was watching *Housewives*.

The janitor's cart was bulky, and it took some maneuvering inside. But when the maintenance person closed the door, she shifted up further in her bed. "Hello," she said.

The man was handsome. Dark hair, olive skin, a strong jaw. As a physical therapist, she noticed he was in good physical shape. When he turned, though, he pointed a pistol at her. She stilled completely.

"Hello," he said, keeping the gun on her as he went to the windows and pulled the blinds. "I'm Johnny Santillo. You might have heard of me."

Of course she had, though this wasn't what she'd expected. He looked nothing like the meth addicts that he'd sent after her. This man was healthy, alert. Cunning.

"Name rings a bell." Her heart had kicked up, racing in her chest. Where were her guards? They'd promised not to go too far.

"The officers?" Santillo peeked through a few slats in the blinds. There was education in the lilt of his conversation. This wasn't a fool. "If you're wondering where they are, Officer Kenner went to the bathroom and might have slipped and fallen. Or I hit him on the head. One or the other. When his partner arrived, he joined him. They're in a closet now. Tied up."

Oh God. How badly were they hurt? "There are other police officers around. You can't expect to get out of here."

"Maybe, maybe not." Santillo smirked. "But we'll see, I guess." He winked at her. "I'm actually waiting for someone."

"Big date?" She had to keep him talking. Her new pepper spray was in her handbag nearby, along with her cell phone. She couldn't reach it right now without giving herself away. She had expected to have a few moments' warning if there was danger. Thinking about it, she realized how ridiculous that was. She should have been prepared, kept the spray closer.

"Your boyfriend is in the parking lot."

Hunter was here. "You've been watching. Waiting."

"Figured it was only a matter of time before he showed up. He'd want to check on you, after the lab explosion earlier." Santillo shrugged. "And I might have mentioned that I was trying to kill you."

She could only blink at him. "You're a psychopath."

"Maybe." Again, the shrug. "But mostly, I spent a few years in jail. It was the worst experience of my life. I've killed people for less. Your boyfriend deserves to die."

"That's horribly morbid." What kind of monster was this man?

"Life's hard, baby. I didn't make my money having sympathy for humanity." That was true enough. He was a drug dealer. She'd witnessed the addicts who had attacked her. Even the woman with the knife. They'd been afraid, out of their minds. Paranoid, probably. Disillusioned.

They'd been promised something and ended up with trouble.

"You scared him so he would come and see me." Of course that's what Santillo had done. Because anyone who had ever met Hunter would know he wouldn't allow someone he cared about to be alone like this. His sense of justice, of righting whatever wrong in his life or in others' lives, well, it oozed out of him.

"I was sick of waiting to finish this. I have a business to run, and I don't have time to keep waiting to get you both in one spot. This isn't the easiest escape plan, but it'll do the trick."

A knock sounded at the door. Santillo waved at her.

She shook her head. No way. If he thought she'd call him in here, he was out of his mind. He could shoot her. Let the chips fall where they may.

He cocked his gun and she only stared at him.

"Charlie?" Hunter's voice sounded through the door as he knocked again. "Hello?"

The blow caught her off guard. She'd been watching the door so intently that she hadn't been paying attention to Santillo.

He hit her across the face with the pistol. It had to have been the gun, because the pain was too much for a fist. There was a pop in her head, and she was sure he'd broken something. Her cheek, maybe. Or her jaw.

She must have cried out, because the door burst open. Through the pain vibrating in her skull, she could only focus on her pepper spray. Unable to see, she dove toward her purse.

Praying, she rummaged on the top, certain she'd left it next to her phone. There. Her fingers closed around it as her vision began to clear.

In front of her, the janitor cart had been knocked over. Hunter had his hands wrapped around Santillo's gun, and they were jockeying for position. The men were evenly matched, but Santillo's hands were on the bottom, right on top of the gun.

She didn't wait. Spraying, she tried to aim for Santillo, but she was certain she got them both.

As both men hit the floor, she reached behind her. Her face throbbed and her stitches pulled, but she pressed the call button and started screaming her head off.

* * * *

An hour later, Hunter sat on Charlie's bed. She held an ice pack against the throbbing bruise on her cheek. The doctor had been in to check it, but he hadn't thought it was broken. They planned to take her to have it X-rayed as soon as the police were finished with her.

Hunter reached for her free hand.

"How are you feeling?" he asked, obviously uncomfortable.

She attempted a joke. "Like a donkey kicked me in the face." She rolled her eyes. "Getting hit in the face with a pistol can ruin a perfectly good day, you know?"

His laugh burst from him, and the sound of it made her grin, too. Except smiling hurt, so she winced. He must have noticed, because his laughter faded, and they lapsed into silence.

Except she couldn't take it. She had too much to say. "Listen, Hunter—"

"Charlie—"

They spoke at the same time. He waved to her. "You go ahead."

"I'm sorry I pepper-sprayed you." She grimaced. "I hear it hurts, but I couldn't figure out how else to help."

He laughed again. "Are you serious? That was brilliant. I couldn't get my footing, with the contents of the cart everywhere. I kept slipping and he had a better grip. It was the right move."

"It was the right thing to make you gag and cough for half an hour?" It had been awful to watch until someone came and assisted him. She wasn't sure what the hospital had done for him, but it seemed to have helped.

"I've been through worse. It stopped Santillo. That's all that mattered." He smiled at her. "You did that. You were a real tough guy."

She dropped her head, tucking her hair behind her ear, sheepish. Then she lifted one shoulder. "I've been working out." She had so many things she needed to say and couldn't figure out where to start.

She must have let the pause go on too long, because Hunter began instead.

"I'm so sorry, Charlie. That coming to see you brought him here. Hell, I'm sorry for getting you tangled up in all of this."

Watching him beat himself up was too hard. She let the ice pack fall to the bed beside her and reached for his hands, gripping them in hers. "I should have been clearer, before. But I'm going to say this now. This isn't your fault."

"Santillo was my—"

"He came after us because he's a bad guy who got what was coming to him. You shouldn't take responsibility for what horrible people do." She rubbed her thumbs over his knuckles. "I get it, though. When I came here, from Chicago, I believed that it was my fault, that I trusted Joshua, that I should have seen what he was truly like under that charming facade. It made me doubt my judgment."

She definitely should take her own advice. Now she could see that she wasn't responsible for what Joshua did. All she'd done was allow herself to care about him. The rest had been his decisions. "But, like Santillo, Joshua made his own choices. And they got what they deserved."

She swallowed, finding it difficult to go on. "But it was my choice to push you away because I was afraid. I'm so sorry." She inhaled, because the rest of this was the hard part, the part that put everything on the line. "I tried to convince myself I was protecting you. But I wasn't. I was protecting myself. Because I love you."

Telling him was like lifting a weight off her. Why hadn't she told him earlier, when she first figured it out? Because she was scared.

She'd been foolish. After all those years watching her parents and their love, how could she have ever believed that loving someone would make her weak?

The smile that broke across his face was sunshine, and she basked in it, letting it warm her up.

Then he kissed her, his mouth achingly soft. She wanted to fall into it, but she still had too much to say, so she pulled back.

"Meg told me that I run because I'm afraid of getting close to people, of sticking around and letting them see me. I don't know if that's true, but I do know that I've been hiding, trying not to be wrong about us, afraid that I was wrong. Because I didn't think I could stand to fail at this."

"We aren't going to fail," he said, smiling. "I'm incredibly stubborn. Haven't you noticed? And I love you, too. More than anything."

She laughed, barely able to restrain the joy racing through her. The words touched her somewhere deep, a place she'd been shielding from the world.

He shifted, coming to sit next to her and wrapping his arms around her. Then he dropped kisses on her forehead, her face, everywhere, until she was laughing and sighing and holding him against her. He gently tilted her head up, careful of her injured cheek, and covered her mouth with his, and though she was in the hospital after multiple attacks, she couldn't imagine anywhere she wanted to be more than in his arms.

When she tried to deepen the kiss, he pulled away, tucking her into the crook of his arm, and she rested her head against his shoulder. Reaching for the ice pack, he gently covered her cheek with it, and she closed her eyes, allowing herself to be with him.

"I can't blame you for wanting to protect yourself, you know," he said, the words rumbling in his chest, under her head. "The things that Santillo has done to you, because of me..." He sighed. "You've been hurt, Charlie. And it's my fault."

"Please stop." When she tried to tilt up to look at him, he held her more tightly against him. So she attempted to put all of her adamancy into her words. "You didn't do that. I need you to believe that. I don't blame you."

He traced circles in her hair, and she wasn't sure if he was trying to reassure her or himself. "How can you forgive me when I'm not sure I'll ever be able to forgive myself?"

She shook her head. Even here, after she'd told him how much she loved him, after he returned the emotion, even then, he couldn't allow that to wipe away what had happened. "Hunter, you carry so much guilt around, I'm surprised you can even stand under the weight of it all."

He chuckled. "Lance said something similar to me earlier today."

"Lance is a smart guy." She sniffed. "Apparently Meg has good taste in both friends and fiancés."

That drew a full laugh from him, and she smiled. "Seriously, though, I'm not sure what else there is to say." She could only offer him her forgiveness. He needed to take it. She couldn't do that for him. "I don't think there is anything else." He inhaled before he went on. "But I think there's something I need to do." This time, she did lift up to meet his eyes. "Oh yeah?"

"It's time I see someone, about my panic, about what's been going on with me this past year. I thought I'd worked through it all. That if I could get myself into shape, if I could pass training, if I could prove to everyone that I was better again, I'd be able to prove to myself that I was fine, too." He bit his bottom lip. "But I don't think I am. And I can't figure it out by myself."

She didn't care how much it pulled her stitches. She wrapped her arms around him, drawing him closer to her. As she laid her head against his chest, hearing his steady heartbeat against her cheek, she smiled. "You don't have to do everything alone, Hunter Buchanan."

"I know." He squeezed her back. "Thank you."

"For what?"

"For loving me, even though I'm not completely fixed yet."

"No one is completely fixed. We're all a little broken." She grinned. "But I think maybe love makes us stronger in the broken places."

He touched her cheek, dropping a soft kiss on her forehead. "I think maybe you're right."

Chapter Twenty

A week after Thanksgiving, Charlie was riffling through some boxes to find her costume jewelry. The dress Meg had chosen for her bridesmaids was deep burgundy, and Charlie was sure she had a set of ruby earrings that would go perfectly with it. But currently they were trapped somewhere in the zillion boxes littering her apartment.

She'd started packing up a month ago, when she'd officially moved into Hunter's duplex with him. Since he wanted to be closer to the air center, in case he was needed, and her job was more flexible, they decided to stay in Redmond instead of at her place in Bend. Not only had her buy-in to the practice been approved, but both Leslie and the other partner had loved the idea of Charlie opening a satellite office in Redmond. Her hours were slowed down while she transitioned, but after the new year, she'd be busy setting up the new place.

Her lease was up at the end of the year. She'd move the rest of this stuff into storage, though, for a few months. They'd already started looking for houses together and hoped to close on something by the time Hunter's lease was up in February. The stuff that she'd left here wasn't necessary, so she could do without it until then.

But because it was a huge disaster, she couldn't find the jewelry she wanted.

Shifting to another box, she unfolded the top to find the remains of her jewelry and the letter she'd been given by Detective Vargas.

The letter from Joshua.

Her hand shook as she lifted it out, staring at her name scribbled across the envelope face in Joshua's compact scratch.

She'd heard from her attorney in the summer that Joshua was still following his theological studies, still living at the seminary. Though initially when she'd heard about his new passion, she'd been dismissive, the longer she spent in a relationship with Hunter, the more willing she was to look forward, not behind.

She hadn't remembered keeping the letter, but obviously she had for some reason. Maybe it was time to see what he wanted. She broke the seal on the envelope and pulled out the single sheet of typed paper.

Charlie,
Please find it in your heart to accept my deepest apologies. What I did to you was inexcusable. I was not in a good place.
In prison, I got a chance to examine my immortal soul and to accept a savior. Through that exploration, I have been able to recognize that my actions caused you great harm. That was not my intention.
I would hope that you have it in you to forgive me.
Sincerely,
Joshua Oldham

She read it twice before lowering the paper to her lap.

She wasn't sure what she'd expected to find in the envelope. Some kind of closure, maybe. She'd figured Joshua would say something, give her some compelling explanation for why he'd done what he'd done. Because of him, she'd uprooted her entire life, had changed her name.

But there wasn't anything in the note in her lap that told her anything she didn't know. He wasn't in a good place? That wasn't an explanation. That was an excuse.

She shook her head, chuckling.

"What's funny?" Hunter stood in the doorway, leaning against the frame. In his tux and the tan he'd gotten over the summer, jumping and fighting fires, he was more handsome than ever.

She held the piece of paper out to him. "Letter. From Joshua."

His brow furrowed, he strode forward, taking it from her fingers and reading it quickly. "Is this new?"

As concern clouded his features, she shook her head. "No. This is the letter Detective Vargas gave me when he told me Joshua wasn't responsible for the break-in."

He read it again as she fished out her earrings and shifted to stand. He offered her a hand so she could step around the boxes in her heels. When she stood in front of him, he whistled low. "You look absolutely amazing."

She leaned up to kiss him, glowing with his praise. Even after all these months, she loved the way he looked at her, as if she were the most beautiful girl in the world. Thanks to the three-inch heels, he didn't have to bend as far to cover her mouth. "Thank you, love."

"Are you okay?" he asked, still holding her in the circle of his arms.

She nodded. "Can you help me fasten this?" She held up the necklace that matched her rubies, pulling the ends around the back and turning around. "Surprisingly, I'm fine. I'm not sure what I expected, but all it has is an excuse and a request to make him feel better. I'm not holding a grudge, and if someone pressed me, I could probably say I forgive him, but I'm not quite ready to make him feel better about it yet."

When she faced him again, he squeezed her shoulders, nodding. "I completely understand. That's exactly how I feel about Will."

Nodding, she leaned forward and let him hold her again.

Hunter had started seeing a therapist right after their tangle with Santillo. He hadn't had a panic attack in almost three months, but he'd also faced some pretty life-changing realizations.

He decided he wouldn't be going back to smokejumping next season. He hadn't shared the decision with many people yet, but he'd told the base manager, Mitch, and a few of his close friends. He'd decided to go to the police academy instead. He wanted to put his life to the service of helping others, but he wanted to do it more personally. His experience with helping the meth cooks turn on Santillo had made a lasting impression on him. He wanted to do more to help people face down those who would manipulate and oppress.

The other huge change was his desire to see his brother.

They'd gone a few weeks ago, to Will's apartment in Portland. It had been incredibly uncomfortable, even angry at times, but ultimately cordial. They'd only stayed for fifteen minutes, but Hunter had insisted on doing it before Meg's wedding. Will would be there, and Hunter didn't want to cause her any stress on her big day. Though Charlie didn't think they'd talk at today's festivities, she hoped the tension was gone. No one wanted to dim Meg and Lance's joy.

She still didn't understand the dynamic between the two brothers. She wasn't sure if Hunter was trying to prove that he was okay now. Or if he needed to see Will, to see if his brother felt any remorse. When she'd asked if he wanted to talk about it, he hadn't. She hadn't pushed. When he was ready to, he would. She trusted Hunter. Either he wasn't sure how he felt yet, or he wasn't quite ready to share.

There was time. Something she'd discovered about them was the quiet certainty that they would have as much time as they needed.

"Are you ready to go?" he asked, offering her an elbow. "You know Meg'll lose her mind if we're late."

Lance and Meg had decided to have a small get-together at a restaurant in Bend. Though Hunter's mother had wanted a larger affair, this being the first of her children to get married, Meg had remained firm. They'd get married next to a lake, in a gazebo, and then have an intimate dinner reception and dancing.

"You look pretty handsome, too, you know." Charlie let her eyes drift over him, from the bowtie down to the shiny wingtips.

He waggled his eyebrows at her. "Think I'll get lucky later?"

"Magic 8-Ball says your outlook is good."

He chuckled. Both Lance and Meg had chosen to have three attendants. For Lance, they were Hunter, Dak, and their colleague Rock. For Meg, they were Heidi, Charlie, and their friend Olivia.

Charlie had helped with some of the touches for the wedding, but Meg had done most of the work. It would be a beautiful evening.

Smiling up at Hunter, Charlie slipped her hand through his arm. "I love you."

"I love you, too." He grinned. "Do you have what you need? We're going home from the wedding."

She squeezed his arm. "I have everything I need right here."

Grinning, they turned off the light in her old place.

* * * *

The wedding was exactly what Hunter expected from his sister and Lance. Intimate, with a lot of laughter. They'd only gone outside for a short time, to do the ceremony. It was snowing today, and though they were covered on the patio, it was still chilly. Being from Oregon, though, the crowd was prepared, covered in wraps and jackets. The bridesmaids, in plaid scarves, looked like something out of a Christmas card.

The restaurant was in a ski lodge. As the holiday season was in full swing, the entire place was covered in twinkling lights, and a fire burned in a big hearth. Outside the windows, snowflakes fell, giving the venue a cozy, tucked-in feel.

Hunter turned a glass of champagne in his hand as he watched his sister and her new husband dance their first dance.

"Thanks." His mother stood next to him, tucking her hand into the crook of his elbow. In a dark green gown, she looked healthy and strong. He wasn't the only one who'd changed over the past year. If his parachuting accident had brought them low, it had also given them the chance to build themselves up again. Now, his mom watched his sister, her eyes shining.

"For what?" He patted her hand, rubbing her cold fingers.

"You gave her away today."

"Of course." He shrugged. "She asked me to."

"I know. But all of us felt your father's absence." She glanced up at him, biting her lower lip. "Thank you for being there." Traditionally, the job should have fallen to Will, but Meg had insisted he do it.

He swallowed and nodded, but he couldn't find any words. With the kind of understanding only a mom could have, she patted his fingers and leaned up to kiss his cheek. "I love you, baby."

"I love you, too, Mom."

His brother watched them. When Hunter caught his eye, Will nodded to him. Next to him, his new girlfriend, Jessica, wrapped her arm around his waist. Hunter had spoken with them both, briefly, and he'd immediately liked her. They'd met in a support group, apparently. Hunter didn't know what the group was for, but his brother seemed less angry than he could ever remember. He didn't say much, but the animosity that used to roll off him was gone.

Hunter wasn't sure how he felt about his brother right now. He'd spoken with his therapist, and she'd told him it was okay if he didn't know. That he didn't have to have all the answers all the time. He was trying to embrace that, to give himself time to sort it all out.

He offered Will a return nod before looking away.

His gaze found Charlie. She was looking at him, and maybe he'd felt her. As always, the instant recognition hit him. His body—his soul—seemed to know her. Across the room, she blew him a kiss. She'd probably seen his exchange with Will and was worrying. He winked in return.

The first dance came to an end, and the DJ said, "Now, we'd like to invite the bride and her brother up for a dance."

Again, Hunter met Will's eyes, and his brother grinned, touching his brow in a salute, giving his blessing and assuring him there weren't any hard feelings.

Maybe things would be okay between them, eventually. But if Hunter had learned anything this year, it was that he needed to take one day at a time.

Swallowing down the emotion, he kissed his mother on the cheek and joined Meg and Lance on the minuscule dance floor.

"Take it easy on my girl's feet," Lance said as he shook his hand. "I've seen you dance before." He smacked Hunter's shoulder good-naturedly, saying all the unsaid things that passed between men in moments like this.

Affection, admiration, some weird humble gratitude for friendship given and received.

He returned the pat. "Whatever, dick. I could have danced better than you when I was wearing a cast." He snorted, and Lance chuckled, his hand at the small of Meg's back.

"Seriously. You guys are trash-talking on the dance floor at our wedding?" Meg rolled her eyes, shaking her head. Her auburn hair was pulled back into a smooth twist of some kind. The style was classic, as was her gown, a no-frills, elegant thing that fell to the floor. But there wasn't anything plain about Meg, with her eyes shining with happiness.

The friends looked at each other and shrugged. "Yes," they said at the same time, and all of them laughed.

Hunter offered his sister his hand. "Come on, Meggy."

As he twirled her out into the middle of the now-empty floor and Lance joined Dak and Rock, Hunter reeled her close, leading her into a waltz.

"Let's show them how this is done," he said, and she grinned. Their father had taught all of them how to dance, pushing the coffee table to the wall in their living room and taking turns with all of them. Some of his earliest memories were of his tall, athletic father twirling his mother around the room. The sound of his mom's laughter still echoed in his mind.

As he and Meg stepped into the old, familiar movements, they didn't say anything, but it was as if they used this time to honor their father, in a moment that should have been his. But there was no sadness between the siblings as they laughed and spun—only joy.

* * * *

"Wow, I had no idea they could dance like that." Heidi sat next to Charlie, watching as Meg and Hunter cut it up on the dance floor. As Hunter dipped Meg and pulled her up into a graceful spin, Charlie shook her head, grinning.

"Me either. But I don't think there's anything the Buchanans can't do if they put their minds to it."

"True enough." Heidi spun her still-full glass of champagne in her hand before placing it on the table behind them.

"Don't like champagne?"

"Love champagne, actually. But…" Heidi paused, glancing around before leaning closer. "Well, I shouldn't drink in my condition." Her lips tilted into a grin.

"Oh my God, you're pregnant?" Charlie hissed, scooting closer in her seat.

Heidi pressed a finger to her lips. "Hush. It's a secret. We didn't want to tell everyone until after the wedding. But we have been working with a high-risk specialist in Portland, and he doesn't think there's any reason I shouldn't be able to carry to term." Charlie remembered that Heidi had lost a child, when she was younger. It must have been worrying her, that her past experience might make it hard for her to have children.

Charlie squeezed her hand, smiling. "I'm so glad to hear that, Heidi. I'm so happy for you."

Her eyes found Hunter as he and Meg finished their dance. For not the first time, she wondered what it would be like to carry his child. She'd always wanted to be a mother, to have a family of her own, but she'd never allowed herself to attach that dream to anyone else before.

Now, though, she did.

Folding her friend into a hug, she squealed. "I'm so happy for you."

"Thanks, Charlie."

"What's going on here?" Dak arrived, handing Heidi a glass. "It's ginger ale." Maybe Charlie imagined it, but he seemed to scan his girlfriend as if taking inventory.

Heidi leaned closer, whispering conspiratorially. "A little bit of nausea."

Charlie jumped up, hugging Dak who, as usual, seemed uncomfortable by the show of affection but touched all the same. "Congratulations, Dad."

"You told her, then?" Dak said, lifting his eyebrows at Heidi.

She shrugged, sipping.

Dak rolled his eyes, but he couldn't hide his excitement. "Now, to get her into a dress like that." He nudged his head toward Meg, who'd found her way back into her husband's arms.

"Wait, what?" Charlie's head was spinning.

Heidi shook her head, waving him off. "I told you. After I'm not afraid I'll spend the day throwing up, we'll talk, pal. And you know you won't catch me dead in a white dress like that." She set her soda down. "The courthouse, small. Just our favorite people."

"You rang?" Hunter stepped beside Charlie, tucking her against him. "You said you're looking for your favorite people? I know you mean me, Heidi."

"To go to Heidi and Dak's wedding." Charlie gazed up at him, unable to contain her grin. "They're only inviting their favorites."

"And apparently that includes you, Buchanan." Dak grinned, offering his hand. "When I can finally get her to schedule it."

"That's amazing." Hunter's face lit up. "Congratulations, you two."

"Right now, I need a walk outside." Heidi had paled, and the smile swept from Dak's face. Faster than Charlie had ever seen someone move, he'd reached down, cupping her elbow in his hand, and hurried her toward the sliding glass door. Dak rubbed her back the entire time.

"What was that?" Hunter asked, circling her in his arms, confusion on his face.

"I think it's what forever looks like," she said, lifting on tiptoes to kiss him.

He shook his head. "I disagree. I'm looking at that right here." Dropping his head, he kissed her, and the music faded as they held each other. "Always."

As they kissed again, she knew she'd found what she'd always wanted...a home here, with him.

Don't miss the rest of this hot series!

TEMPT THE FLAMES
and
CRAVE THE HEAT

Available now
Wherever ebooks are sold
From Lyrical Liaison

Meet the Author

Award winning author and RITA® finalist Marnee Blake used to teach high school students but these days she only has to wrangle her own children. Originally from a small town in Western Pennsylvania, she now battles traffic in southern New Jersey where she lives with her hero husband and their happilyeverafter: two very energetic boys. When she isn't writing, she can be found refereeing disputes between her children, cooking up something sweet, or hiding from encroaching dust bunnies with a book.

Stay connected with Marnee by signing up for her newsletter at: http://www.subscribepage.com/marneeblake.

Find Marnee on the web at www.marneeblake.com, on Twitter @marneeblake, or on Facebook at www.facebook.com/AuthorMarneeBlake/.